# The Princess Who Flew with Dragons

Also by Stephanie Burgis

*The Dragon with a Chocolate Heart*
*The Girl with the Dragon Heart*

# The Princess Who Flew with Dragons

## STEPHANIE BURGIS

BLOOMSBURY
CHILDREN'S BOOKS
NEW YORK LONDON OXFORD NEW DELHI SYDNEY

BLOOMSBURY CHILDREN'S BOOKS
Bloomsbury Publishing Inc., part of Bloomsbury Publishing Plc
1385 Broadway, New York, NY 10018

BLOOMSBURY, BLOOMSBURY CHILDREN'S BOOKS, and the Diana logo
are trademarks of Bloomsbury Publishing Plc

First published in Great Britain in August 2019 by Bloomsbury Publishing Plc
Published in the United States of America in November 2019
by Bloomsbury Children's Books

Bloomsbury books may be purchased for business or promotional use.
For information on bulk purchases please contact Macmillan Corporate and
Premium Sales Department at specialmarkets@macmillan.com

Library of Congress Cataloging-in-Publication Data
Names: Burgis, Stephanie, author.
Title: The princess who flew with dragons / by Stephanie Burgis.
Description: New York : Bloomsbury, 2019.
Summary: Twelve-year-old Princess Sofia of Drachenheim enjoys freedom from her sister's
manipulations during a diplomatic mission to far-off Villenne, until she and her dragon friend,
Jasper, are forced to face ice giants.
Identifiers: LCCN 2019004268
ISBN 978-1-5476-0207-0 (hardcover) • ISBN 978-1-5476-0208-7 (e-book)
Subjects: | CYAC: Princesses—Fiction. | Sisters—Fiction. | Dragons—Fiction. |
Magic—Fiction. | Giants—Fiction. | Fantasy.
Classification: LCC PZ7.B9174 Pri 2019 | DDC [Fic]—dc23
LC record available at https://lccn.loc.gov/2019004268

Typeset by Westchester Publishing Services
Printed and bound in the U.S.A. by Berryville Graphics Inc., Berryville, Virginia
2 4 6 8 10 9 7 5 3 1

All papers used by Bloomsbury Publishing Plc are natural, recyclable products
made from wood grown in well-managed forests. The manufacturing processes
conform to the environmental regulations of the country of origin.

To find out more about our authors and books visit
www.bloomsbury.com and sign up for our newsletters.

For Patrick Samphire, my partner in every adventure.
I love you even more than dragons!

# CHAPTER 1

I *knew* it was a bad idea to leave home even before I ever heard about the ice giants. But when your older sister rules your entire kingdom, it's almost impossible to say no to her.

"Sofia! Good morning." My sister, Crown Princess Katrin of Drachenheim, gave me her warmest smile as she greeted me from her seat behind the polished wooden desk of her office.

*Oh no.* I'd seen too many powerful nobles take their seats under the spell of that smile, only to be sent away fifteen minutes later with stunned faces, somehow persuaded into plans they could never have imagined in their worst nightmares. It had been six months since the last time Katrin had come up with a clever new plan for *my* life. The very idea of being drawn into another one now made me want to flee straight back to my bedroom, to curl up with the protection of books and a locked door.

I was a princess, though, and princesses can never show fear. So I crossed my arms and scowled, planting myself firmly in place. "Well?" I demanded. "What is it this time?"

Her eyes narrowed dangerously. "I beg your pardon?"

I narrowed my own eyes back at her even as nerves rattled frantically against my chest, reminding me of every battle I'd lost against her before. "You've summoned me to your office instead of your sitting room," I told her impatiently. "That means we're here on business—there's something you want me to do for you. But you're sitting behind your desk instead of coming around to meet me. *That* means you know I won't want to do it—so you're reminding me that you're the one in charge." As *always*.

"Hmm." Katrin's lips tightened. One long, elegant brown finger tapped twice on the desk. Then she stilled it and her face relaxed into its usual serene authority. "Well," she said, "apparently I haven't wasted the kingdom's money by hiring those expensive tutors of yours."

Now she was complimenting my intelligence.

I was in so much trouble.

I said, "Please tell me you haven't promised me in marriage to a wicked fairy *again*!"

Her perfect jaw tightened. Her voice sounded as if it were being ground through glass. "I never actually signed that betrothal contract last winter."

But she'd seriously considered it, and we both knew it. My sister might have been forced to take on the duty of raising me when our mother died, but I'd always understood what mattered most to her:

*Anything for the good of the kingdom.*

I raised my eyebrows pointedly. "How about that time you sent me up to the top of a clock tower to be eaten by monsters?"

"I did *not—!*" She stopped and let out a long, controlled breath. "I was forced to send you as a *hostage* to attacking dragons, not as their *supper*. If you recall, it was our only chance of saving the city! But those 'monsters' have become our kingdom's best allies ever since we signed our treaty with them. Didn't you just send a five-page-long letter to one of them yesterday?"

"Hmmph." Of course her spies told her whenever I sent Jasper a new letter. The fact that my one true friend was a dragon who lived underneath a mountain over sixty miles away—and wouldn't even be allowed to leave his cavern until he turned fifty—meant our letters were the happiest and easiest space I knew. We would never meet, so I would never have to worry about mucking things up, the way I always did in person.

But I should have known that our letters had never been truly private. Even in the apparent safety of my own rooms, I was surrounded by ladies-in-waiting at all times . . . and naturally, I wasn't the one who had chosen them.

My sister was all about *control*.

*Control of her emotions*, which she never allowed any of the rest of us to glimpse anymore . . . *if* they still existed and hadn't been swallowed up like everything else in her life by . . .

*Control of the kingdom,* which our father had handed over to her several years ago. He hadn't wanted to deal with any difficult decisions—or any emotions of his own, either, after our mother's death. Something had vanished behind his blue eyes when Mother died, leaving only a hearty, artificial veneer that I could never manage to pierce.

*And, of course, control of me.*

"I trust," she said evenly, "that you will *always* wish to do what's best for our kingdom, no matter what the personal sacrifice might be. Is there any other repayment for what our people give us?"

She waved one graceful hand at the luxurious office around us, full of rich, dark wood and gleaming silver. "This palace . . . these lovely gowns we're both wearing . . ." She tilted her head. "Have you just put through *another* order of new books from the university at Villenne?"

I tried not to squirm. "So?"

I'd been forcing myself to save most of my pocket money for other purposes lately—but this was a brand-new series of tracts by my favorite philosopher in the entire world, Gert van Heidecker, taken from his famous lectures in far-off Villenne, and it looked utterly *amazing.* I couldn't wait to curl up with all six volumes on my bed and close the door on the rest of the world while I absorbed every one of them from beginning to end. I might not even come out for meals until I'd read them all at least three times through.

It was the one time I ever felt completely confident that I was *definitely* doing the right thing: when I was lost in a beautifully impractical, passionate debate over the nature of truth or free will or reality itself, with my imagination flying free and the terrifying outside world locked far away from me.

Philosophy was all about the search for wisdom—a search that could take place without any interruptions in the safety of my own bedroom. Better yet, I could argue anything I liked when it came to philosophical debates, because for once, I couldn't hurt my family *or* my kingdom with any of my stupid mistakes or strong opinions—and in the study of philosophy, unlike courtly life, we were *supposed* to argue over everything.

It was absolutely perfect for me.

"I saw the price of those books, Sofia." Katrin's voice pierced my happy fantasy. "Do you have any idea what most girls your age earn as a salary each year, in their full-time work as apprentices or housemaids?"

*Ouch.* I set my teeth together.

The awful truth was, I *hadn't* known that a year ago. It had never even occurred to me to wonder. Six months ago, though, I'd seen for myself the way refugees lived on our city's riverbank, sleeping in thin tents even in the snow. All of them scratched out a living with their makeshift market— even the youngest children there.

I'd met fierce, brave girls my own age, too, who were working hard for their living. Unlike the unobtrusive servants in our palace, *they* hadn't been shy about letting me know what it felt like.

Last winter, two of them had saved my life and the entire kingdom from a fairy invasion that had left me with nightmares ever since . . . and the worst part was, I'd done almost nothing to help them along the way. I'd always dreamed of showing my sister that I *was* worthy of our family after all—but when the real test had come, I had stuttered and stumbled and had to be *rescued*, like a helpless—no, a *useless* princess.

I'd always known I was a disappointment as a royal. But I'd never realized how disappointing I was as a *person* until then.

Katrin's tone gentled as I stood in scowling silence. "I know about the money you've been sending to the riverbank to build real houses there."

"So?" My shoulders hunched. "They deserve roofs over their heads, don't they?"

It was the least I could do from the warmth and comfort of my rooms. But I'd tried so hard not to let my ladies-in-waiting find out. No *one* was supposed to know that I was the one funding those houses.

I should have known better than to think I could keep any secrets from my sister.

"I agree," she said calmly. "Unfortunately, there's been some unrest among the city's merchants. They claim the new construction would spoil the view from their shops—and you know how much they hate that riverbank market! However, I dealt with their objections rather neatly in yesterday's privy council meeting. In fact, we're *all* delighted that you're finally taking an interest in our city."

*Uh-oh.* I eyed her suspiciously, hugging my arms tighter across my chest. I knew that purring tone of voice.

"What would you think," she asked, "of *not* having those books shipped here from Villenne after all?"

*Oh no.* Righteous fury boiled up within me. *Not this time!*

I had been out-manipulated by my sister so many times. But this was going *too far.*

The words ground out between my teeth: "That money came from my personal allowance, Katrin! I have *every* right to spend it on books—"

"And of course you can still buy your little books," said Katrin soothingly. "But you needn't have them shipped all the way here after all."

"I . . . beg your pardon?" I blinked, caught off-balance.

My sister sat back, lacing her hands on her lap and cocking her head, like one of my many tutors waiting for me to fail another unexpected test. "You may not have heard," she said, "but there is a great and historic exhibition about to take place in Villenne."

"You mean the Diamond Exhibition?" As if she could catch me out that easily! I'd had tutors in everything from etiquette to astronomy flinging unexpected quizzes at me every day of my life. "Of course I've heard of it, Katrin. It's in all the newspapers."

"Well, it is a once-in-a-lifetime event." Katrin's smile deepened. "The chance to view the greatest inventions, magical spells, and industrial offerings of our age, all gathered together on display . . . It sounds worth a royal look-in, don't you think?"

7

I stared at her. "Katrin, Villenne is over four hundred miles from here, and that exhibition begins *this week*. Unless you've learned how to fly—*oh*."

*Oh no.*

Of course humans couldn't fly themselves, without wings. But I *had* flown once before, veering wildly back and forth through the night sky on the scaly back of Jasper's ferocious sister, Aventurine, as she and her best friend had saved me from invading fairies and goblins, leaving my family's palace broken and burning behind us.

That whole night was a memory shrouded in horror—one that I never, ever wanted to repeat. I'd barely even left my own room ever since. If it were up to me, I would *never* step outside the rebuilt walls of our palace again.

But I should have realized that my calculating older sister would remember all the details from that night and reshape them into a use that I could never have imagined.

*Oh, Katrin.*

I'd been trying so hard to stay fierce and strong throughout this meeting, but at the thought of my sister's slim, upright body sailing out of reach, so high and vulnerable in the sky above me . . .

I sank down into the chair in front of Katrin's desk. "*You're* going to fly there?" I asked in a horribly small voice.

*My sister* was going to fly hundreds of miles away from me? Out into the terrifying, unknown outside world where *literally anything* could happen?

My sister, who kept everyone and everything in this kingdom under control, was planning to *leave*?

*Never.*

"You can't leave Father to look after everything!" I straightened triumphantly in the chair. "He would never agree to that. Anyway, you know he would make a terrible muddle of the kingdom while you were gone."

"I know." Katrin nodded approvingly. "That's why *you*, Sofia, are going to fly there in my place to represent our kingdom. We need someone to represent us to the wider world, to find us new trading partners and allies from across the continent. If you can manage any of that, you'll win our merchants' full support for those houses on the riverbank.

"So, if you want to help our people, collect your precious books, *and* finally prove your value to the kingdom . . . !"

She smiled sweetly as I gaped at her in disbelief, an empty hollow forming inside my chest where my silly, unearned sense of security had rested ever since our palace walls had been rebuilt.

"Isn't it lucky," said my sister, "that you've already flown once before?"

# CHAPTER 2

Needless to say, my devious older sister didn't give me any time to think up an escape. Within less than an hour, I was sitting in a beautifully ornamented wooden carriage—one of my family's finest!—as it rose straight up into the air from our southwest courtyard, dangling from the giant claws of a massive green-and-gold dragon: Jasper's terrifying aunt Émeraude.

It wasn't that I didn't like his family . . . in theory. But it was *so much* easier to like them from a distance of sixty miles or so.

Katrin smiled serenely as she waved her farewells from the safety of the paved ground below, where she stood next to our big, bluff, red-headed father. He had already finished waving and was beaming around at the gathered courtiers now with his usual, meaningless public smile. I'd hoped to snatch a moment in private to beg for his help, but he'd only strolled out at the last minute and given me a quick, bruising hug that muffled every protest I'd tried to make.

Then I'd been bundled into the carriage with my ladies-in-waiting all rustling and chattering after me . . . and our guards had shut the door firmly behind us.

Wind gusted against the doors and windows as the dragon's giant wings beat above us, sending our carriage swaying in midair. My two younger ladies-in-waiting, Anja and Lena, shrieked with excitement as our view of the golden palace veered sickeningly up and down.

The two guards who accompanied us looked stern and unmoved. My older lady-in-waiting, Ulrike, was already working at her embroidery with her usual aggravating air of prim self-righteousness, blonde hair piled in perfect curls above her head.

I took deep, slow breaths through my clenched teeth and tried with all my might to calm my roiling stomach.

"Aaaah!" The carriage took a sudden, swooping dip, and my stomach swooped with it. A horrible moan escaped my lips before I clamped them shut and squeezed my eyes shut, too, against the nauseating view of all those houses below . . . much, *much* too far below us.

"Isn't this exciting?" Anja bounced happily up and down on the seat beside me, tilting the carriage more every time she moved. "I never imagined that I would fly!"

Oh, for goodness' sake. "You're *not* flying," I muttered, slitting my eyes half open to glare at her. "*That's* the dragon."

And it was utterly humiliating. No matter what I tried—no matter how many promises I ever made to myself—my sister always outwitted me in the end.

Gert van Heidecker wouldn't have let himself be so easily outmaneuvered. He won philosophical debates across the continent every year and left his opponents shriveled and mumbling in defeat. I'd read all the details in his published letters, and Jasper and I agreed: he was the ideal philosopher.

... The ideal *human* philosopher, anyway. Jasper insisted that the finest dragon philosophers were even more impressive. But when he found out that I had bought Van Heidecker's newest treatises hot off the press, I knew perfectly well he would snort smoke in envy.

It was almost enough to reconcile me to this trip . . .

. . . Until the carriage took a sudden, sharp swing to one side and my stomach lost its battle with gravity.

*"Urrrrp!"*

My sister's guards really were well trained. They didn't budge so much as a muscle as I was sick all over their polished boots.

Anja and Lena did, though. They both shrieked with horror as they yanked their feet out of the way, and Lena's face turned positively green.

It was the only comfort that I found in that whole day's journey.

We finally sighted Villenne forty-eight unspeakable hours later. By then, my silk gowns were hanging noticeably looser around my figure and my head was pounding an endless, throbbing beat. I'd managed to eat a few scraps of food each night when we'd landed, but each time I'd gotten back into the carriage, I'd lost everything I'd eaten the night before.

With every breath, I cursed my sister's scheming. The amusement in our dragon's golden gaze both nights, as she watched me stagger around on legs like loose jelly, didn't sweeten my mood either. Not even a long new letter from Jasper—tossed carelessly in my direction from Émeraude's great claws—could make me feel any better. He'd written to me in big, sloping dark red ink.

*I only wish I could be there with you to explore the most famous human city in the world! Just think: you'll be exploring the city of Gert van Heidecker himself! You must tell me everything about it.*

But all I could think of were the stories his aunt Émeraude would carry back to him about me. They would all be unbearably humiliating. Jasper and I had formed a perfect philosophical friendship by letter—but could it actually survive if he discovered how useless I was in real life?

Ugh.

Even Lena and Anja looked unusually subdued as we all took our places for our third day of travel. No number of washes could clear the stench from the carriage by that point, and the glass windows had been sealed for flight. They couldn't be opened without breaking them.

Every one of us had tried.

But as the third hour of flight began that day, something nigh on miraculous occurred. High, round, colorful domes shaped like curling seashells appeared in the distance below us.

A gleaming white palace rose up from the center of the shimmering seawater beyond . . . and the older guard, Jurgen, spoke for the first time in our whole journey. "Villenne." He jerked his square brown chin at the window in a nod. "That's it, Your Highness."

"*Uhh!*" A croak of pure joy escaped my throat as I lunged forward to spread my fingers against the glass. It felt blessedly cool against my skin. The sight below felt even better. I took it in with a greedy gaze, absorbing every detail as we swung back and forth above it and my stomach lurched in accompaniment.

Somewhere down there, in that massive cluster of islands connected by sparkling white bridges, was the university where Gert van Heidecker lectured to enraptured students in serious blue robes.

Somewhere, too, was the Diamond Exhibition, the reason I'd been forced into this carriage of horror in the first place.

But most importantly . . .

Somewhere down there was a bed—a *real* bed, with a mattress and a deep, cozy duvet, in a room with a door that actually *locked*. Soon, I would be tucked underneath that duvet with my brand-new books and a steaming pot of hot chocolate in my hands. I could hardly—

"Move aside!" Jurgen barked as he and the younger guard jerked upright in their seat across from me.

"I beg your pard—!" I began.

He yanked me away from the window as something round and black shot past it.

Screams filled the wildly rocking carriage. I didn't join them. I just absorbed the message of that cannonball with pure, cleansing fury.

"They're shooting at us," the younger guard, Konrad, announced.

"Of course they are," I snarled.

*Thank you so much, Katrin.*

Enough was enough.

Ignoring my guards and ladies-in-waiting alike, I grabbed the door handle and flung the carriage door open in midair.

# CHAPTER 3

Cold wind rushed into the swinging carriage. I gripped both sides of the doorway for balance, leaned outside as far as I dared, and bellowed:

*"You flaming idiots! Don't you know who we are?"*

The carriage shook suddenly harder, and I staggered. An ominous rumbling sound exploded above me, making me flinch—until I realized: giant Émeraude was actually laughing.

I glowered up at her green-and-silver belly. "And just what are *you* amused by?" I shouted.

Her long, scaly neck snaked down through the air until her massive head was grinning directly at me with dozens of long teeth fully bared. "*You*, little princess," she said in a voice like thunder. "I find you amusing."

Another cannonball *whooshed* past me, less than a foot from my head. I tightened my grasp on the doorframe, resisting my guards' attempts to pull me back into the carriage. "Have you even noticed we're being *shot at*?" I demanded.

Émeraude's great green lips pulled back even wider, revealing impossibly more teeth. "My scales are impenetrable," she said with malicious satisfaction. "They can shoot as many pebbles at me as they like. I'll take no notice."

"Gaah!" I stomped my foot in frustration—and the carriage tipped, throwing me forward.

"Aaaahhhhh!" Desperately, I clung to the doorway, my feet dangling in midair...

And my guards landed with twin *thuds* against my back.

I fell forward, screaming. My arms windmilled in the open air, but there was nothing there to save me.

The connected islands of Villenne spread out far below, strange and lovely, the last sight I would ever see...

...Or so I thought, until something much worse appeared before me.

"No-o-o!" I twisted desperately, but gravity was inescapable.

I fell directly into Émeraude's open mouth and landed in hot, stinking darkness as her massive jaws closed around me.

Everything blurred in a fog of horror and disbelief.

*Nonononononononono—!*

Sunlight pierced the darkness. Emeraude's great, hot tongue curled beneath my body. I was tipping, tumbling, falling...

And I landed on the wooden floor of my carriage a

moment later, panting and staring up at the horrified faces of my companions.

"Ahhh—ahh—*ahhh!*"

I slammed my mouth shut. But I couldn't stop the desperate wave of shivers that shook my body against the floor.

The smell of the dragon's mouth clung to my skin and my hair. My hands and gown were sticky from her tongue.

I had *been inside a dragon's mouth!*

"Your Highness?" Lena peered down at me, blue eyes wide. "Are you all right?"

I stared up at her in disbelief.

Was I *all right?*

"She should really have a bath," Émeraude said through the open doorway, smacking her lips. "She tasted like sick. Disgusting."

*That was it!*

I pushed myself upright. Breathing hard, I grabbed hold of the closest bench seat and pulled myself the rest of the way up until I stood on wobbling legs.

"*Tell me,*" I said to Jurgen. "Did my sister bother to warn the Valmarene royals that I would arrive with a dragon?"

"Er . . ." Jurgen gave a sidelong look at our dragon, whose green-and-silver face still filled the doorway. "I believe she thought it would be an effective show of strength, Your Highness, for that to be unexpected."

"An *effective show of strength.*" My teeth clenched on the words. "And did she have any ideas about how we could stop our hosts from thinking they had to *defend themselves against fiery death* when we arrived, out of the blue, with a terrifying *dragon?*"

He cleared his throat, looking pained. "She . . . gave me to understand she had discussed that matter with Lady Émeraude's family." He glanced again, even more nervously, at her. "I believe there was meant to be a flag? To assure our hosts that we come in peace?"

Émeraude snorted, her hot breath swirling through the carriage. I shuddered uncontrollably at the too-familiar smell of it.

"I don't care for carrying silly flags from my mouth," she informed us disdainfully. "And I am not a citizen of your puny kingdom."

"Oh, for . . ." As another cannonball flew past our unbroken window, I let out a growl fierce enough for any monster. "Fine!" I snarled. "I'll do it myself, then!"

So that was how I entered the fabled city of Villenne on my first-ever diplomatic mission: hanging halfway out the open door of my carriage, with dried dragon spittle covering my hair and my skin and my two guards gripping tightly to my legs as I dangled a heavy Drachenheim flag in midair.

It was a good thing I'd never expected to be the perfect princess for this mission . . . because this had to be the most embarrassing first impression *ever*.

When we finally landed on Villenne's central island, swooping low over the glittering blue water that surrounded it, dozens of black-robed battle mages were waiting for us. They stood in tight, martial lines, framing three edges of the large tiled square between the great white palace and the water. Near the back of the square stood a couple draped in silks and furs who must have been the king and queen of Valmarna ... but six more rows of armed soldiers stood between them and us.

Every one of them looked poised and ready to leap into action the very moment we chose to attack. It might almost have been funny if I hadn't been fighting so hard to keep myself from being sick again in front of all of them.

Émeraude dropped the carriage the last few feet onto the ground with a *thunk* that bounced me off the floor and cracked my head against the open doorway. Grinding my teeth, I pushed myself up, letting the flag fall from my hands and kicking my legs free from my guards. I could feel every eye in the square watching me, and it made every inch of my skin burn with horror.

I *hated* looking stupid. I hated it *so much*! But because I'd been born on royal display, someone was *always* watching me whenever it happened.

So I jerked my chin into my haughtiest pose, as if I didn't care at all, and patted down my spittle-sticky silk gown while my ladies-in-waiting fussed behind me and clucked despairingly about my hair. There was nothing that could be done about that without a bath or, better yet, a pair of shears. I would have shaved my entire head just to be free of that dragon-mouth-stink!

But right now, it was time to act like a princess for the sake of my people, my kingdom, and my own trampled pride.

Lifting my disgusting skirts, I stepped as gracefully as I could from my carriage...and every soldier before me yanked up their muskets in challenge.

I froze. My guards lunged from the carriage to throw themselves in front of me.

The sound of Émeraude's laughter rolled ominously through the air...and I finally realized that those muskets were all pointing up at *her*. She had dropped down just above us while I'd been focused on my own humiliation, and her wings cast a cool shadow over the tiled square.

"You needn't worry, puny humans," she rumbled down to us. "I'm not hungry for any delicious little snacks like you today. I only wished to say farewell to my valued ally." She tipped her massive chin at me, her golden eyes glinting, and lowered one scaly eyelid in a wink. "I've enjoyed these past few days, young one. I look forward to meeting you again."

I glowered at the malicious amusement in her gaze. "We thank you for your kindness," I growled, "and look forward to meeting you again, as well."

*But only in my nightmares*, I finished silently.

By the look in her eyes, she knew it. Chortling, she circled low over the square as the soldiers' muskets tracked her, waiting. Then she shot high into the sky, sending a gust of cold wind billowing over all of us in her wake.

*Phew.* My shoulders relaxed for the first time in days as I turned to the royal couple before me, shifting my guards aside and ignoring all the soldiers who still stood between us. Five minutes of empty compliments on both sides, and I'd be *finished* with this unbearable journey at long last! I'd be conducted to my guest room in the palace, I'd take a luxuri-antly long, hot bath, and then I would *finally* be left alone to snuggle up in warm duvets with my new Gert van Heidecker books and—

"*Well!*" King Henrik's bushy gray mustache quivered with fury as he strode toward me, scattering soldiers in his wake. Small and skinny, he was barely two inches taller than me, but his chest swelled impressively as he swaggered to a halt much too close to me for comfort. "This was *not* the courtesy we expected from a guest, young lady!"

*Argh.* All my instincts warred against my training. "Your Majesty," I began tightly, "if you would simply—"

"Are you actually attempting to order *me* around? *You?*" He raked his gaze over me, lips curling with open disgust. "If you are a princess of Drachenheim," he spat, "*which* I *doubt,* then what *exactly* do you have to say for yourself? I can only hope, for the sake of your insignificant little kingdom, that you have come prepared to grovel for your behavior *and* your most inappropriate appearance!"

*That was it.*

I had never groveled to anyone in my life—and if this man thought he could stand here and bully me, he had *no idea* of what I'd already endured.

I had *been inside a dragon's mouth*!

So I raised myself up until I was looking directly into his glaring eyes and smiled fiercely as I said, "I beg your pardon. Did no one ever bother to *tell* you we had allied with dragons?"

In royal-talk, of course, what that actually meant was: *Your spies must be terrible! How sad for you.*

His face flushed bright red. "You impudent little—of course we *knew* of your cursed alliance! But to fly over our capital city with no warning—"

"Oh no, were you *frightened*?" I cooed with gooey, sickly sweet sympathy. "Oh, dear. We're such good friends with dragons ourselves, you see, we sometimes forget that other, *weaker* kingdoms might fear them."

My younger guard, Konrad, gave a convulsive cough beside me that made his lanky body shake. Jurgen thumped his skinny back with one big hand as the king's face shifted from dark red to dusky purple.

Who knew that diplomacy could be *fun*?

Before King Henrik could actually explode from fury, though, his tall, silver-haired wife glided up behind him, resplendent in deep purple silk and an ankle-length silver cloak. "Forgive us, Your Highness," Queen Berghild said sweetly, "but we were *so* taken by surprise by your magnificent entrance, I'm afraid your proper quarters aren't ready for you yet."

"Oh?" My whole, bruised body sagged as my vision of bath, bed, and books slipped even further out of reach. "I'm sure I could make do with—"

"No, no." The queen heaved a sigh of almost-perfectly faked regret. "You see, the room we'd originally assigned to your party would never do, now that we've met you. Those quarters in our palace are *far* too small for a princess who is *such* good friends with dragons!"

Hmm. I narrowed my eyes up at her suspiciously. "And the quarters that *would* be appropriate?"

"Oh, those won't be ready for at least another week . . . or maybe three. Possibly not until the Diamond Exhibition is long over." A triumphant smirk stretched Berghild's lips. "Luckily," she added in a kind, motherly tone, "we have quite a pleasant little terraced house set aside for moments when such *honored* guests arrive without warning. Better yet . . ." Her eyes widened. "It's a good forty minutes away from here, so you won't be distracted by any of our nation's *inferior* entertainments or royal gatherings."

"*Forty minutes?*" My voice came out as a croak. Suddenly I could feel every piece of dried dragon-spittle on my gown and in my hair as if they were burning directly into my skin.

"Forty minutes," repeated the queen with deep satisfaction. "First by boat, and then by carriage. I should warn you, though, the boat journey can be a bit unsettling." She glanced at my spittle-stained gown and her smirk deepened. "I do hope you don't get travel-sick?"

Behind me, Anja let out a groan of horror.

For once, I couldn't even blame her.

From: Her Most Exalted Highness Princess Sofia Alexandrina
Maria of Drachenheim
85 Svëavagen
Gemlarna
Villenne

To: Her Most Exalted and Serene Highness
the Crown Princess
Katrin Augusta Sibylle of Drachenheim
The Royal Palace
Drachenburg
Drachenheim

Dear Katrin,

~~Well~~

~~As you may have predicted~~

~~You won't be surprised to hear~~

~~Next time you expect a dragon to follow human instructions~~
~~or logic~~

. . .

~~I wish~~

~~I'm sorr~~

Never mind. I'm sure you know what happened already.
You always do. So I don't know why I even tried to write
this letter.

# CHAPTER 4

*Thump!* I thumped my pillow as hard as I could.

*Thwack!* I threw myself down on top of my narrow bed and crossed my arms tightly, locking myself in.

This was exactly what I'd been longing for, wasn't it? The chance to lie in a comfortable bed without interruptions?

*Fwoosh!* My abandoned letter to my sister fluttered off the writing desk and landed on the rug beside me like a cream-colored accusation.

I squeezed my eyes shut as laughter floated through the floorboards from the salon below. Were my ladies-in-waiting all laughing together about just how badly I had mucked this mission up? I'd been sent here to prove my value to my kingdom, and instead I'd gotten myself expelled to the middle of nowhere in this shabby, doll-sized house. Half the rulers of our continent were meeting at that beautiful white palace to eat and dance and forge nation-changing alliances . . . and I wasn't invited to join any of them.

Even my new books were sitting in the palace without me.

I rolled over onto my stomach and buried my face in my pillow with a groan.

It was one thing to fail myself—or even to fail my sister. I was used to both of those. But to fail everyone else who needed me . . .

Would Katrin really give in to the merchants' demands and tear down those new houses on the riverbank only because I'd been an idiot? *Surely not.* She'd always said our most vulnerable people's welfare had to be our highest priority.

But then, she'd also always said that I had to live with the consequences of my actions.

*This* was why it was better to stay locked in my room, back home, with my books. Whenever I left it, *bad things happened.* And now—

**Rattle rattle rattle!**

That sound was coming from the windows. Was this whole house going to fall apart in the wind?

"Argh!" I pushed my face deeper into my pillow.

"*Mrow!*"

My head jerked up.

Two wild green eyes stared expectantly at me through the window. One brown-and-gold paw batted impatiently at the glass.

*Rattle rattle rattle!*

I stared back in astonishment. It was an actual *cat*!

I'd caught glimpses of them before, but only through my carriage windows. They prowled through the crowded streets of Drachenburg like miniature tigers in a moving jungle of human legs. I'd never understood how so many people could ignore those clawed and dangerous creatures slipping so close to their ankles.

But this one was looking straight at me—and demanding to be let inside.

This whole day had been surreal beyond belief. So I slid off the bed, padded in my stockinged feet across the floor, and had already begun to swing open the window before my mind finally surged into action.

"Wait!" I stopped as fresh air slapped my face . . . too late.

"*Mrow!*" The cat sailed past my shoulder in one long leap and landed, outrageously, *on my bed*. It didn't even look nervous, or ashamed of its own behavior! It padded arrogantly around and around the duvet, investigating the pink-and-white-striped covers with a skeptical sniff. Then it sprawled across the mattress like a throne and turned back to gaze at me with a superior air.

Its pointed ears twitched. A loud rumbling noise emerged from deep within its body.

Was it *threatening* me now?

"You must be joking," I told it. "I've dealt with dragons today. Do you think *you* can intimidate me?"

Its mouth opened wide in a disdainful yawn, displaying

startlingly sharp teeth. Its silver claws flicked in and out on my bedcovers warningly.

"I was in a dragon's *mouth*," I informed it, and crossed my arms.

The cat's eyelids lowered in obvious disbelief.

On a normal day, I would have called a maid to deal with it. On a bad day, I might have even screamed for a guard.

But after everything that had happened earlier today, I couldn't bear to face any of my entourage right now. So I strode across the floor to the bed and glowered down at the ferocious small animal who lay in wait there as it looked back up at me, ears swiveling ominously.

"Well, cat?" Bracing myself, I stuck out one threatening finger. *Don't even think about those sharp claws!* "Are you going to leave my bed by yourself, or do I need to—*oh!*"

The cat lifted itself with one swift, sinuous stretch to firmly push its furry, brown-and-gold head against my hand. As my fingers loosened with shock, it rubbed against my skin again and again in almost . . . a *stroking* motion. Was it actually trying to cuddle?

Its fur felt warm and astonishingly soft. As I stared down at it, wordless with disbelief, that low, rumbling sound began once again. This time, it didn't feel so ominous after all.

Could that be . . . *purring*? That was what cats did when they were happy. I'd read about it in a book once, long ago.

But why would it be happy to be petted by *me*?

Slowly, carefully, I lowered myself onto the narrow bed. I held my breath as I settled in beside my feral, sharp-clawed visitor.

Purring even louder, it shifted over until it was nestled against my side, a warm, soothing pillow that shifted beneath my hand with the steady rising and falling of its breath. I stroked my fingers tentatively along its back, braced for it to turn and strike with its pointed teeth at any moment. Instead, it stretched out luxuriantly, lethal claws flexing in and out against the covers.

Petting it felt . . . *good*. Startlingly good, actually. Almost against my will, I found myself curving even closer.

Royal families didn't cuddle—or at least, my family didn't. I couldn't imagine Katrin ever cuddling *anyone*. My father had given me that unexpected, brisk hug before my journey, but he'd barely even looked at me as he'd given it. In my memories, my mother had been warm and kind, and I had known she'd truly loved me . . . but still.

I wasn't the sort of person anyone would ever *want* to cuddle.

. . . Except, apparently, this cat. As I lowered my full body onto the bed, it plastered its furry body tightly against my chest and stomach, purring loudly, until it finally fell asleep fifteen minutes later.

Something hot pricked behind my eyes as I looked down at its utterly relaxed body, so boneless and trusting in my arms. Snuffling snores replaced its steady purr.

Had anyone *ever* trusted me that much before?

I remembered the contempt in the king of Valmarna's eyes as he'd looked me up and down, visibly cataloging every spittle-stained inch. "*If you are a princess of Drachenheim, which I doubt . . .*"

I had known all my life that I was a failure as a princess. Now the rest of the world finally knew it, too. *So many* people had been watching me today! Everyone across the continent would read in the papers about how terrible I really was as a diplomat and a royal.

And yet . . .

Not *everyone* thought I was awful, did they? This wild little animal in my arms didn't know I was a princess. It was the first creature I'd ever met who didn't even care about my family or my obligations. It just liked snuggling up to *me*, for some inexplicable, miraculous reason.

As I stroked my fingers through its lush, soft fur, its trusting warmth seeped into my chest like magic, easing muscles I hadn't even known were knotted . . . and I found my eyes straying again and again to the window it had come through. The sky shifted slowly to darkness outside.

There was a whole city out there, stretching far into the horizon. No one in those busy streets had ever seen me before. Just like this cat, they wouldn't know I was a princess if I didn't tell them.

What had Jasper said in his letter? *I only wish I could be there with you to explore the most famous human city in the world!*

Was I really going to write back and tell him that I was locking myself away from all of it only to hide in my own room? After all the embarrassing stories his aunt was already carrying back to him about my travels with her? Jasper might be a philosopher, but he was a dragon, too. He would never understand if I was a coward. He might even be so disgusted by it that he would never write to me again.

The outside world was terrifying and unsafe. I had learned that lesson six months ago. And yet . . .

The fairies and their horrifying goblin guards were all safely underground in Elfenwald now, hundreds of miles away from Villenne. Maybe the rules actually *could* be different here.

I'd already failed my official mission. But perhaps . . . if I could only find the bravery to try . . . I might prove myself to be a worthy friend for a dragon after all.

I stroked the golden-and-brown miniature tiger who'd leaped into my room from the outside world like an invitation.

*Tomorrow,* I promised myself as the cat snored against my chest, *things are going to be different.*

# CHAPTER 5

The next morning, the cat leaped neatly back out through the window after sharing my breakfast and indulging in one final, purring petting session. I looked wistfully after it as it padded off gracefully over the curving rooftops.

If only I could escape so easily!

The maid who worked in this house didn't know me well enough to be startled when I rang for her to help me dress at a shockingly early hour. But when I walked through the doorway of the salon downstairs, where my ladies-in-waiting were gathered around a low table eating breakfast in their dressing gowns, they all jerked to their feet, napkins fluttering to the floor.

"Your Highness!" said Ulrike. "You're awake!"

"And dressed!" Lena's eyes widened.

"And *here!*" Anja finished with unmistakable horror.

"Shh!" Lena hissed, and Ulrike gave her a warning look.

*Too late.* I scowled at all of them, my shoulders tightening. Who cared if they didn't want me around? I'd never wanted to be with them, either—and I could finally do something about it.

"I only needed to tell you that I'm going out," I said curtly, and turned back toward the door.

"What?"

"Where?"

"*Wait!*" That was Ulrike; she hurried across the room, skirts swishing, to block my way. "Your Highness, if a message has arrived from the palace—"

"That's not where I'm going." Setting my teeth, I waited for her to move.

"The Diamond Exhibition, then? Where all the other royals will be?" Plucking at the sleeve of her dressing gown, Ulrike glanced back at the younger ladies-in-waiting. "It might be wise to give the queen more time to recover her temper first, but if you're determined on it—"

"*Not* the exhibition." I sighed. "I couldn't get anything done there with the queen set against us! Think about it logically, Ulrike: we're in Villenne. The greatest city in the world! Even *dragons* are excited by the sound of it. There must be *some* other neighborhoods in this city that I can explore without bumping into her."

"But . . ." Ulrike blinked rapidly. "Your sister's instructions—"

"Failed," I finished with a snap. "That's why we're here

now! And I am *not* going to sit in this dingy little prison just *waiting* for that horrible, smirking Queen Berghild to take pity on me!"

Ulrike winced, edging backward. "Perhaps, if you wrote and apologized to Her Majesty—that is, explained . . ."

"Apologize? To *her?*" I barked out a harsh laugh. "I'm leaving. Now. I'll be back by tonight." *Or in less than an hour if I lose my nerve,* I admitted silently to myself. My palms were dampening with sweat, and my heartbeat rattled against my chest.

But none of them needed to know how cowardly I really was. So I pushed past Ulrike and hurried down the narrow, creaking wooden staircase before she could witness the panic in my expression.

Konrad popped into view, tall and skinny and startled, at the base of the stairs as Ulrike's anguished voice called down after me: "Your Highness! We haven't even summoned your carriage from the stables yet! You cannot go wildly adventuring around this city without a plan. Your sister—"

"—*Isn't here,*" I shouted back. "Which means that—for the first time ever"—my pulse pounded as I whirled around to face my oldest lady-in-waiting—"*I'm* in charge of what I do while we're here. Aren't I?"

Ulrike gaped down at me. "I . . . But . . ."

Heavy footsteps sounded behind me. "Your Highness," Jurgen rumbled. "Perhaps . . ."

"Well?" I demanded, looking back and forth between the two adults. "*Aren't* I?"

"We-e-ell . . ." The word dragged itself out of Ulrike's

mouth. "Of course you *are*, Your Highness, but you know your sister would say—"

"Ulrike," I said grimly, "because of my sister, I've been sent hundreds of miles away from home, been made sick in a flying carriage, and been shot at by our hosts! The *one* advantage of being here now is that I am the *only* princess of Drachenheim in this entire country. So all that matters here is *my* command. If you disagree?" I narrowed my eyes up at her. "Then you can go straight back to Drachenburg and explain everything to the crown princess yourself."

There was a long, echoing silence. The narrow stairwell seemed to close in around me, tighter and tighter with every moment. If she called my bluff—if my nerve broke . . .

Ulrike let out a puffing sigh. "Very well, Your Highness. I will summon your carriage."

My shoulders relaxed, but I shifted from foot to foot impatiently. "How long will that take?"

"Half an hour," Konrad volunteered. "The stables are fifteen minutes away, at a good run."

"Then I'll walk." I stepped off the final stair and started purposefully for the front door.

"But Your Highness!" Ulrike bleated behind me. "The dirt—the crowds—"

"Other girls manage to walk through large cities every day," I told her through gritted teeth. "If they can do it, I can, too." *I will not shame myself again.*

"We'll keep her safe," Jurgen promised Ulrike.

"Wait a moment." I frowned as he and Konrad both stepped forward to flank me. "Shouldn't at least one of you stay here? The others are staying, and they'll need protection, too, so—"

"*Protection?*" Ulrike let out a trill of high-pitched laughter. "From *what*, Your Highness? We're in no danger without you!"

I stared up at her, speechless.

"*We're* not the ones who could earn a kidnapper a fortune," she told me with bitter clarity. "Do you have *any* idea, Princess, just how much of the kingdom's treasury your sister would have to empty if you were caught and held for ransom? Or how Drachenheim would suffer once winter came if that money had been spent?"

*Ohhh.* Sickness coiled in my belly as I imagined it. All those families on the riverbank . . .

I frowned, yanking my imagination back under control. "This is nonsense. No one even knows I'm here! I was supposed to be at the palace with the other royals. How could any kidnappers even guess who I am?"

Jurgen coughed pointedly.

My cheeks heated as Ulrike shook her head at me pityingly. "Your Highness, have you actually *seen* what you are wearing?"

Frowning even harder, I glanced down at my gown. It was a mix of thick, beaded brocade and silk, and it was a perfectly pleasant shade of rose pink. "So?" It wasn't exciting— I'd never taken much notice of any of my gowns—but the maid had done up all the buttons and hooks, and I couldn't see anything scandalous about it.

Ulrike sighed and swept one hand along her own lilac

dressing gown. "Can you see the difference in the quality of our attire?" she asked. "Take a moment. Look at the materials. And then think of what those *other* girls on the street outside will be wearing."

She shook her head grimly as I thought that through. "Two soldiers aren't nearly enough, Your Highness. The truth is, it will *never* be safe for you to walk in an open street without a full honor guard to protect you ... for the sake of your protectors *and* your kingdom."

"Oh." My voice came out as a strangled croak as misery sank through me.

She was right.

Here I was, hundreds of miles from my sister's watchful eye for the first—and possibly last—time in my life ... and my *clothes*, of all the most pointless items in the world, were about to ruin my only chance to find out who I could be without a crown.

*Do not cry!* I sucked in a fierce breath through my nose, forcing back the stupid, pointless tears. With Ulrike's watchful gaze on me, I clenched my jaw shut.

It didn't matter how miserable I felt. Like it or not, I *was* a princess. I couldn't risk my guards' lives—or my kingdom's treasury—just so that, for once in my life, I could feel free.

I stepped onto the first stair without another word.

Then Anja called out from behind Ulrike, "I could lend the princess one of my gowns!"

*What?* My head jerked up.

Ulrike whirled around, shooing Anja further back, out of my sight. "Don't be absurd!" she snapped. "Her Highness will *not* wear any of your gowns. It would be shockingly inappropriate and—"

"You two *are* the same size." Lena peeped around Ulrike's shoulder to look me up and down critically. "If we don't pull the laces too tight around the waist—"

"Enough!" Ulrike said shrilly. "The princess would *never, ever* agree to—!"

"The princess," I said, "would absolutely *love* to."

For the first time in ages, a smile stretched across my face.

Of course a princess couldn't walk through the streets of fabled Villenne with only two guards to protect her. But a girl who *wasn't* a princess—an ordinary girl with two guards walking close by just in case . . . What *couldn't* she do?

I couldn't wait to find out.

# CHAPTER 6

Half an hour later, the outside world hit me like a full-body slap.

How could everything be so *dirty*? Grime was everywhere—*people* were everywhere, shoving and crowding past our doorstep and yelling back and forth to each other. No one even made space around the door of our house as I opened it into the chaos.

There were crowded streets in Drachenburg, too. But I had driven through those in my family's carriage, with thick panes of glass, gilded wood, and armed outriders keeping everything and everyone safely at bay.

Here, the noise and the smells all rushed in on me at once. All those yelling voices battering my ears—and the *stench!*

I stopped short on the edge of the doorstep, my head spinning. I yanked my gaze down to try to keep my balance, but even that didn't help. The front doorstep was made of some strange, dark gray stone that I'd never seen before. The sight made me feel even more sickeningly out of place. Everything I knew spun further and further away from me as my breath shortened into rapid pants.

Ulrike was right: I didn't belong here.

I should have known—

I should have *never*—

"Your Highness?" Jurgen's voice broke through my whirling thoughts.

With a gasp, I jerked my head up—and up—to look at him properly for the first time since we'd met three days earlier.

His broad, dark brown face was set in perfectly neutral, professional lines ... but the sympathy in his brown eyes and in his deep, rumbling voice was impossible to miss. "We can still turn back if you'd like," he said gently.

*Ugh!* Humiliation burst through my chest as I suddenly realized what kind of picture I had made, standing frozen and staring on the doorstep for so long.

Konrad was younger than Jurgen and not as good at keeping his own thoughts off his pale, freckled face. He looked torn between pity and horror, and the sight made my spine straighten with a snap.

"What a perfectly ridiculous suggestion!" I glared down my nose at both of them. "I was only getting my bearings!"

Chin up, I stepped off the front doorstep and onto the

pavement . . . where my slippered foot immediately landed in something soft and gooey.

*Ewww!*

I bit my tongue to keep myself silent and strode forward into the pandemonium, squelching grimly.

The next few minutes were a blur of jaw-clenching, brute determination as I forged my way through the thick mass of people. Heavy baskets slammed against my legs. Strange hands waved so close to my face that they nearly knocked me over. No *one* made way for me, ever—but when my guards shifted forward to defend me, I waved them back with a meaningful glower.

Konrad and Jurgen had changed into plain, off-duty clothing, with their swords hidden under knee-length brown overcoats. As far as anyone else could tell, they were ordinary citizens who just happened to be walking near me. If they started intimidating innocent passersby out of my way, it would draw far too much attention to all three of us—and attention was the one thing I truly couldn't afford.

So I surged fiercely forward, lowering my head like a battering ram. I didn't know where I was going, but I didn't care. I just had to keep moving and *not give up.* I *would not* be defeated by the crowd or by my fears. I would—

"*Out of the way!*" Something short and blue hurtled so close in front of me that I stumbled back, gasping. My guards hurried forward, but my attacker was long gone, leaving a whole path of stumbling, complaining people in his wake.

One woman, just past us, hissed the word like a curse: "*Students!*"

*Students?*

With my two guards flanking me, I strained my eyes and finally saw it: the flicker of a blue robe through the crowd. Of course! All the students in Gert van Heidecker's classes at the University of Villenne wore robes, didn't they? I'd seen them pictured in lithographs at the front of his bound lectures.

They sat in beautiful marble lecture halls wearing floor-length blue robes to cover up any sign of where they'd come from, because while they were students, for that one perfect moment, they were all equal partners in the pursuit of knowledge. And while I devoured Van Heidecker's printed words long after he'd spoken them, they heard his own magnificent voice for themselves.

They could ask him questions, and *he would answer*. They could express their opinions and debate the meaning of the world without fearing what might happen if their opinions weren't correct. They could get fierce and angry and even bellow if they liked, because philosophers were *supposed* to be passionate in their debates. Students were *supposed* to develop real opinions, not just smile and mouth the practiced words that would be safest for their kingdom.

Student life was everything I'd ever dreamed of—and everything hopelessly out of my reach. The rules of my life had been drilled into me from the day I was born.

A younger princess was to marry well and bear

children when she was older. She was to smile at public ceremonies through her life and keep her true thoughts safely to herself. Whenever she was witnessed by the public, she was to judge her words with care, keep her appearance tidy and pleasing, and *never* offend anyone, no matter what the provocation.

It was why I had always had to have all my lessons on my own, without any other students to join me—and why I'd known that I could *never* attend university, no matter how desperately I wanted it.

"That ... that ..." Konrad swallowed visibly as he stared after my not-an-attacker. "That was a g—I mean, did you see? I think—I'm almost certain that was a—"

"Student," I finished for him. "Come along!" I strode forward without waiting for any answer, ignoring the agitated, distracting muttering I heard between him and Jurgen in my wake.

It was a good thing Lena had reminded me to bring a pouch of gold coins on this morning's expedition. All three of us were about to acquire beautiful sky blue robes of our own ... because I knew *exactly* how to use my once-in-a-lifetime freedom after all.

CHAPTER 7

Jasper was going to be *so* jealous! As I took my seat two hours later on a long, splinter-filled wooden bench near the back of a slanted, narrow lecture hall, I planned out every delicious detail to include in my next letter.

Walking into the ivy-covered Philosophy Building had felt like an initiation into a mysterious and secluded secret society. But then, the whole university felt like a magical world of its own. It covered an entire small island where no carriages or horses were allowed. To reach it, my guards and I had had to cross a narrow, arching white stone bridge that shimmered in the sunlight. It was crowded elbow-to-elbow with hurrying, blue-robed students and pushy street vendors who shouted nonstop while white gulls cawed and circled overhead.

"Essence of Amberdine to enliven your essays!"

"Notepaper so thick, you can use it twice!"

"Enchanted ink to enspell your exams! Pass every course without an hour of study!"

That last sales pitch had made me stop and frown. "It isn't possible to enchant ink, is it?" I'd whispered to my guards.

I knew about battle mages and music mages. I even knew one single food mage, Jasper's grouchy sister Aventurine, who used her magic to transform between dragon and human forms—and was equally impossible in both shapes. *Ink* mages, though? My tutors had never mentioned those.

"It's a fraud, Your Highness," Jurgen murmured quietly. "Most of these vendors are selling false wares."

"Are you sure?" Konrad's blue eyes looked bigger than usual in his freckled face. "Everything's topsy-turvy in this city. I *tried* to tell you earlier, I'm sure I saw—"

"Aha!" I'd *finally* spotted a stand selling secondhand student robes and caps. I strode toward it as triumphantly as any of my ancestors conquering a new kingdom. "Perfect," I declared.

And we did blend in perfectly a few minutes later as the wave of blue-robed students swept us up in its midst and carried us off the crowded bridge onto Scholars' Island.

*Scholars' Island!* The name was amazing. And the place—! Everywhere I looked, I saw ancient brick buildings devoted to the pursuit of *knowledge* instead of power or gold. Everywhere I looked, I saw blue-robed students—sprawled atop the long stone benches, seated with their backs against the big oak trees, or lying on the grassy lawns before each building.

Some were reading, scribbling notes, or debating; others hurried in and out of the buildings, balancing piles of books in their arms.

There was just one thing that they all had in common: full-length sky blue robes covered all their clothes and jewelry. No one could tell by looking at them who any of their families were, because while they were here, *it didn't matter.*

It was astonishing. No, it was a miracle. For the first time in my life, I felt almost . . . *comfortable.* Was this how other people felt all the time? As if they *weren't* standing out like a sore thumb, just waiting for everyone else to notice how wrong they were?

I could have wandered around those leafy squares forever. I might have, too, if it weren't for the notice I found plastered on the back of a bench twenty minutes later: *Today's Lectures: Gert van Heidecker on The Nature of Power, Part II, Philosophy Building, Auditorium B . . .*

Thank goodness I'd followed that gorgeous cat's lead and dared to come out on an adventure! I laughed out loud with wonder as I traced my fingers over the letters on the page. "*Finally!*" I told my guards, ignoring their baffled looks. "Something's going right after all!"

And to think: if I hadn't offended that haughty queen, I would have been trapped in tedious conversation with other royals right now. I didn't care if my sister betrothed me to a *dozen* wicked fairies in punishment for my rebellion! This taste of happiness was worth anything.

And I was still glowing with the truth of that as I sat waiting for the lecture to finally begin in the windowless

lecture hall I'd hunted down in the far back of the Philosophy Building. This might not be the pristine marble auditorium that I'd expected from the lithographs in front of Van
Heidecker's books, but that made it *even better*. I was discovering something new, something I never could have learned
back in Drachenburg!

And since no enemies would ever expect to find a princess of Drachenheim on an uncomfortable wooden bench
surrounded by commoners . . .

The door behind me slammed open, and my guards
scrambled up from the bench on either side of me, reaching
in unison for the swords hidden beneath their student robes.
"You see?" Konrad hissed. "I *knew* I'd seen a goblin!"

*Goblins*. There had been *so many* goblins in my palace on the
night of the invasion six months ago. They'd served the fairies
who had tried to drag me underground to force my family
into compliance. For all their evil, those fairies had been shining and beautiful, their true menace hidden behind their
gorgeous, inhuman glow. But their secretive goblin guards . . .

I hadn't even realized they were in our palace until it
was too late. Lurking in the shadows with their murderously
long knives, dark red caps, and long, sharp teeth stained with
blood . . .

One of the girls who'd saved me had managed to bargain with a goblin guard along the way, but their alliance
had been so dependent on clever word choices and trickery,
I'd barely breathed the whole time that he'd stood nearby.

The way his knife had glinted by his side as my palace burned...

"I am not a *goblin*," said an insulted voice behind me. "Haven't you ever seen a beautiful kobold before?"

The words were so unexpected, they broke through my trance.

That had been a girl's voice.

My guards were still struggling to pull their swords out from their all-encompassing layers of clothes as I turned and found three squat, green-skinned goblin girls in blue robes flanking a smaller, scowling fourth girl the size of a five-year-old human. She glared up at us with bright blue eyes under bushy blue eyebrows. Her long, ghost-white ears stuck out sideways at least four inches in both directions under her plain blue student cap, and her long, loose, snow-white hair fell down around her robe like an icy waterfall. I'd never seen anything like her in my life.

She certainly wasn't a goblin—and even the others didn't look like the goblin guards who'd served the fairies of Elfenwald. Not only were they dressed as students, but I couldn't spot a single blood stain on any of their sharp white smiles. Only a long, skinny, peppermint-striped sweet stuck out from the wide mouth of the goblin girl at the far end. She kept sucking on it slowly as she grinned up at us with her robed arms crossed—a sight so disrespectful and so shockingly improper that my deportment tutor would have swooned.

But I found myself infinitesimally relaxing.

"A kobold?" I could finally move and think again, so I waved my guards down. Heads were turning all around us. No one else seemed frightened by the new arrivals, but too many people were looking at us.

"Obviously." The kobold girl snorted, and a puff of cool blue mist blew out of her pointed white nose. "Do I *look* like a goblin to you?"

"Ha!" said the goblin girl with the peppermint sweet. "You should be so lucky!"

"We're not *supposed* to talk about where we come from at all." The middle goblin girl spoke with prissy care, her green nostrils flaring. "We're on Scholars' Island, remember? None of that even matters. No one cares who or what anyone else is anymore."

The other two goblin girls and the kobold traded one expressive glance ... then burst into shrieking, jangling laughter that broke like jagged glass through the tension in the room.

"All right, shove over." The kobold strode forward, miniature elbows jutting outward. "Come on!" she added impatiently as I stared at her. "We all have to squeeze in somewhere, don't we? So if you don't want us sitting on your laps through the lecture—"

"How *dare* you?" Konrad gasped. "If you think—"

"Of course!" I jumped to my feet, poking him hard in the shoulder. *Princess Sofia* moved aside for no one, as a point of principle, but Princess Sofia couldn't be here today ... and these were the last creatures in the world who could ever be allowed to learn my true identity. "We'll make space," I promised.

"Your H—my lady." Jurgen lowered his voice to a whisper as he leaned over me. "Perhaps it would be best to attend a different lecture today. Or—"

"A different lecture?" The goblin girl with the peppermint sweet shook her head at him as she settled comfortably onto the bench beside me. "Don't be ridiculous. Old Heid-y's about to get dragged off in chains. If you leave now, you'll miss all the fun!"

"*Chains?*" I repeated blankly. Konrad tried to push between us, but I nudged him impatiently out of the way. "What are you talking about?"

"His arrest, of course." She rolled her eyes, sucking harder on her peppermint sweet and propping her elbows on the long desk shared by everyone on our bench. "Don't you know anything? That's why it's so crowded here today. All the upper students have been laying wagers outside the library on whether he'll punch a royal guard when he's taken. I have five krügen on him tripping at least two of them on his way down."

"Pah." The kobold snorted as she threw herself down onto the bench. "It'll never happen. The man's tiny!"

"Oh, I've been studying him." My goblin girl narrowed her dark eyes thoughtfully. "He may be small for a human, but he's feisty."

"But . . . this is absurd!" I shook my head in disbelief as I looked between them. "Gert van Heidecker is the most admired philosopher in the world! Why on earth should he be arrested? *No one* would ever dream of—"

"Aha!" The goblin girl beside me pulled the peppermint sweet from her mouth and used it to gesture toward the bottom of the room. A small, bald man wearing oversized spectacles and an outrageously bright orange coat stepped behind the battered-looking wooden lectern, fussily adjusting several pages of notes. "There he is, right on time. And now . . ."

Her large green ears swiveled like bat wings underneath her cap to point toward the door. I heard what she was listening to a moment later: booted feet marching down the corridor toward us.

I knew that sound. I'd heard it many times before, back home.

*Soldiers.*

I exchanged a wild look with my guards. What was going on?

They were already starting to their feet.

"We must go." Jurgen seized my arm in a firm grip. "*Now*, my lady. Before—"

"Too late!" As the door to the lecture hall crashed open behind us, my goblin neighbor bit down on her peppermint sweet with a satisfied *crunch*. "Now the show's finally ready to get started."

# CHAPTER 8

Twelve armed soldiers in black-and-silver uniforms marched into the lecture hall and lined up against the back wall. Sharp swords glinted at their sides.

Didn't *any* of these people understand that Scholars' Island was a haven of peace and knowledge? For goodness' sake, even *horses* weren't allowed here. How could they need weapons?

"They're blocking the door." Jurgen sank back down onto the bench beside me. "We can't get past them now—unless . . ." His voice lowered to the thread of a whisper as he leaned close. "If we tell them who you are—"

"Don't you dare!" If I got myself publicly mixed up in an arrest, my sister would throttle me. "This is just a misunderstanding. It has to be."

"Nope!" said the goblin girl beside me. "Just look at his face!" She nodded at Gert van Heidecker, who was glowering at the soldiers through his spectacles. "He's not planning to back down, is he? And the king issued a public warning yesterday—if Heid-y goes through with his planned lecture, he's heading for prison, and he knows it."

"For a *philosophy lecture?*" Konrad demanded incredulously.

"Oh, don't worry." She winked. "He'll have help on his side. Half the people here are planning to pile in and defend him as soon as the guards make their move."

"What?" My incredulous gaze crisscrossed the room full of blue-robed students. None of them held anything but pens or books in their hands. "But—"

She flipped up the wide blue sleeve of her robe to reveal a whole stash of piled sweets tied to her muscular green arm. "It's amazing what you can cover up under one of these." She slid a meaningful look at my guards, whose swords were once again safely hidden underneath their own robes. "I only came to eat and enjoy the spectacle . . . but your two friends here aren't the only ones who've snuck more dangerous toys along with them."

Jurgen hissed out a curse I'd never heard before, his strong jaw squaring purposefully. "That's it! My lady, you *cannot* allow yourself to be caught up in a riot. Your sister—"

"Ahem!" Gert van Heidecker barked from the front of the room. "Ladies and gentlemen . . . and honorable *guests.*" His powerful, rasping voice turned into a snarl as his gaze fixed on the line of impassive soldiers at the back of the room. "We are assembled today in pursuit of a better world. We shall not be silenced by those who fear the truth! The rulers of our continent may be blinded by power and greed, but *our minds* are our own, and they may never be chained!"

"Argh!" Jurgen tipped his head into his hands with a groan of despair, while Konrad simply stared, open-mouthed.

My sister was going to cut off my pocket money *forever*. But since it was too late to leave now, I leaned forward on the bench to catch every single word.

*No one* had ever talked this way in front of me. Not ever!

"The rulers of half a dozen nations are gathered at our city's Diamond Exhibition at this very moment, enjoying the fruits of our people's labor as if it belonged to them by right of birth . . . and with as much pride as if *they'd* made any of those grand discoveries themselves." Gert van Heidecker lingered on those final words with disdainful emphasis.

"Of course we all agree those inventions are remarkable. How can we not? With these new advances in technology, we will be able to create astounding new settlements in the iciest extremes of the frozen north, where no human has ever dared to go before. Incredible though it sounds, our rulers claim that our astonishing new weapons may soon render us fearless of the legendary ice giants themselves! So the Valmarene kingdom will spread farther and farther across the globe, heedless of ice and snow and giants alike . . .

"But who, may we ask, gave our royal family the right to claim credit for the hard labor on display, while they drape themselves in jewels and finery and never lower themselves to a day's work in their lives?"

*Ouch.* I couldn't help wincing at that question, my shoulders hunching defensively as murmurs of approval sounded around the hall. Perhaps I did have some inkling, after all, of why the king of Valmarna had forbidden this lecture. Not that I *approved* of arresting philosophers, but . . .

"As we come to the question of royal pride, let us ask ourselves: what *is* the true goal of this Diamond Exhibition?" Van Heidecker tilted his head at an inquisitive angle. "Our rulers *say* we must dazzle the world with a display of our growing power. They *say* nothing else can prevent those greedy rival kingdoms with their terrifying dragon allies, their assembled battle mages—and even the monstrous ice giants of the north themselves!—from descending upon our wealth and good fortune like vultures at a stolen feast.

"But is that truly the explanation? Perhaps, here in the sanctum of Scholars' Island, this great nursery of the mind . . ." He gave a pointed look over his spectacles at the grim-faced soldiers who lined the back of the lecture hall. "As students of human nature, we may ask ourselves: *would* our rulers really develop so many expensive new weapons unless they actually *hoped* to use them? And: how long will it take them to use those weapons *on their own citizens*, if we dare protest a future filled with endless imperial expansion and war?

"So we return to the question of last week's lecture: what is the nature of true power? Different philosophers have defined it differently across the ages, but every one of them has finally agreed: *power only exists when wielded over other people.*"

An ominous clanking sounded behind me. It was the noise of twelve armed soldiers stepping forward all at once—and drawing their swords. Gulping, I twisted around and found their captain glaring down the slanted aisle at Gert van Heidecker, one big, gloved hand raised in unmistakable warning.

But the world's most famous philosopher stuck up his small chin in defiance as he continued, holding the captain's gaze fiercely: "Thus, I submit this week's great question: *What is the difference between a rightful king and a tyrant? And when, exactly, are a ruler's citizens allowed to stand up and cry out as a nation: We reject your authority over us?*"

*Oh no.* My jaw dropped open.

This wasn't just philosophy anymore. It was *revolution.*

"Gert van Heidecker!" The captain's voice rang out through the lecture hall. "I arrest you in the name of the throne!"

Shouts broke out across the room, desks overturned, and my outspoken goblin neighbor was proven right: these students had come prepared underneath their plain robes. An awful lot of them had brought weapons . . . and some of them were *unbelievably disgusting.*

"Ewww!" A stinking projectile whizzed past my face, and I ducked only just in time. More and more of them flew through the air all around me, like a nightmarish shower of muck. They might have been aimed at the soldiers who were marching down the aisle, but that didn't stop something sticky from landing on my cap.

"Uggh!" I shook my head frantically, throwing my arms

up as a shield. This was *not* what I'd expected from my first philosophy lecture!

Maybe I didn't want to go to university after all.

My guards' swords snicked free as they leaped to their feet beside me, but there was nothing they could do against the rain of stink. I would have cowered underneath the long desk, but it had already been shoved over by a group of students on the far end, while the goblin girls and kobold on the bench beside me shared out their stashed sweets among themselves and shouted sarcastic commentary on the action, their feet swinging casually in midair.

"Come on, you can do better than that!"

"Aim for their *heads*, dummy!"

I slid off the bench to huddle onto the floor with my arms thrown over my head. But then I heard something worse: the clang of swords.

Real fighting had begun.

"That's enough!" The captain's bellow rose over all the yells and confusion. "Bar the doors! *Everyone in this room* is now under arrest!"

*Oh no.* Nausea roiled through my belly.

This couldn't be happening!

When the awful king and queen of Valmarna realized that I'd been a part of this . . . I curled forward into a rocking ball of panic.

When the news of my arrest broke in all the newspapers—!

"Right!" the goblin beside me said cheerfully. "That's our cue, girls. Come on!"

A strong green hand closed around my arm and yanked.

I stumbled to my feet, thoughts whirling as I met the goblin girl's fierce grin. "What? *What?*"

"Unhand the p—unhand her!" Konrad bellowed.

"Oh, certainly! Be my guest." Rolling her eyes, she let go of me. "If you *want* to go to prison with all the rest of them—"

I grabbed her robed arm without a second thought. "What are you—?"

"Shh!" She nodded firmly at my guards. "Now grab her shoulders!"

Their large, warm hands closed around me, anchoring me in place as the world spun around me in a haze of stinking rain and surreality.

This had to be a nightmare. It couldn't be my life.

"Hurry up, then!" snapped the tiny, blue-eyed kobold, tapping one bare foot impatiently. Beyond her, the other two goblin girls were chatting happily to each other as they held the kobold's thin shoulders, looking perfectly at their ease and utterly oblivious to the chaos tearing the room apart around us. "What are you waiting for, a signed invitation? Honestly! *Humans.*"

Shaking her head in exasperation, the kobold closed one small, blue-nailed white hand over my goblin girl's broad shoulder, completing the chain of connection along both of our combined groups . . .

And together, all seven of us vanished.

# CHAPTER 9

I could never have explained how I ended up tumbling down a set of dark, creaking stairs into an underground coffeehouse ten minutes later, as part of a jostling, noisy group made up of three outrageous green goblin girls, two stunned-speechless human guards, and one extraordinarily vain little kobold...

...Without a single word of protest. I didn't even try to get away!

It was completely inexplicable.

We weren't invisible anymore; we didn't need to be. All the chaos was taking place in the Philosophy Building, while the rest of Scholars' Island was untouched—and the goblins' coffeehouse was well hidden beneath the massive ivy-covered university library, which had looked so grand

and noble in my earlier tour of the island. I'd never imagined, in my first admiring walk around that building, that there was actually a secret trapdoor hidden beneath a large boulder nearby; or that when you tapped on that door with just the right kind of knock, it would swing open to reveal a set of mossy stairs leading down to the wildest place I'd ever been.

It was a good thing I wasn't Princess Sofia right now, because she would never in a million years be allowed to visit anywhere so loud or dirty . . . and it was absolutely *fascinating!*

Faintly glowing blue-and-green moss covered the damp stone walls of the secret coffeehouse, which was lit only dimly by a dozen or so fat candles guttering on the makeshift tables. I had to squint to peer through the shadows around me—but then, most of the creatures here didn't need candles anyway.

Who knew so many goblins were making merry beneath Scholars' Island? I spotted at least two dozen scattered across the cavernous room in student-blue robes and caps, their green hands wrapped around massive clay bowls of steaming hot coffee as they argued and shouted with laughter. They weren't the only creatures here. Three tiny kobolds sat at a nearby table, strange blue sparks flickering around their long, skinny white fingers as they scarfed down sugarcoated buns that smelled enticingly like cinnamon. And in the far corner, hidden in the deepest shadows, I could just barely make out a strangely shaped, hulking statue . . . *wait.*

"Is that a *troll*?" I blurted.

The goblin girls stopped talking to stare at me. Then they burst into shrieks of laughter.

"You should see your face!" My neighbor wrapped one strong arm around my waist with a companionable squeeze that made me jerk with surprise. "Don't worry. Old Abjörn's been asleep for thirty years so far. I don't think he's going to wake up now just because he smells a few humans!"

"He doesn't eat humans anyway," said the prissy goblin girl beside her. "Or at least, I *think* that's what I heard." She frowned thoughtfully. "Or was it just that it's been a *long time* since he ate them, since he's been asleep?"

"Either way!" The goblin girl beside me pulled me along by my waist all the way to the closest low table—a collection of three wooden crates haphazardly stuck together.

I didn't dare glance at my guards as I let her nudge me down onto one of the fat cushions that surrounded the makeshift table. My skin was still tingling from the shock of being touched like that by anyone—with such familiarity and ease, as if I were a *huggable* sort of person. Apart from that one brief, suffocating hug from my father just before I'd been bundled into the flying carriage, no one except for last night's cat had touched me with affection for as long as I could remember.

It had felt . . . well, actually . . .

Of course, it was a *shocking* imposition. If I *were* Princess Sofia of Drachenheim, I would never dream of allowing it!

. . . And yet, somehow, I didn't feel offended at all, not even when the other goblin girls and the kobold crowded so close around me that the sleeves of our robes brushed together across the table. I tucked up my legs on my cushion with shameless impropriety, folded down the heavy skirts of my dress to make room for the others—and looked eagerly to the squat counter in the far corner of the room, where a couple of fast-moving goblins were taking orders.

"The best coffee you'll ever find," said my neighbor. "So much better than that slop the humans serve aboveground!"

"Do they have any hot chocolate?" I asked hopefully.

"Chocolate?" She let out another ear-jangling shriek of laughter. "Who do you think we are? Royalty?"

*Oops.* I should have remembered that chocolate was an expensive luxury for most people. "I just . . ." I jerked my chin up defensively. "I'm not from here," I muttered.

"Well, *obviously!*" She dug one pointy elbow into my side, making me gasp with shock. "You should have seen me when I first got here. Straight from the mountains, I was—almost as far north as the ice giants' palace! It must've been at least a month before I stopped gaping at everything like a cave worm."

"You still do, Talvikki." On her other side, the kobold smirked. "The only difference is, nowadays, every time you gape, that ridiculous peppermint sweet falls out of your mouth!"

"Ha!" Talvikki popped the sweet out of her mouth and flung it directly at the kobold's face.

I jerked back instinctively, ready to run—

But the kobold girl was laughing, too, as she snatched the sweet from midair. "Mmm. Yummy!" Her shockingly vivid blue eyes flicked up to my two guards, who were still hovering warily behind me. "If you two aren't planning to sit down, why don't you go ahead and order for all of us?"

"Order?" Konrad's pale eyes widened in the candlelight. "From *them*?"

His gaze darted toward the counter, where the two goblin owners leaped back and forth, scrambling up and down shelves with careless ease. They grabbed and flung cups and plates, drinks and cakes with astonishing, inhuman speed.

"Here," I said, and dug out the purse that Lena had insisted I bring with me. "I'll pay for everyone."

They had rescued us from arrest, after all. The thought of my narrow escape made me sag with relief as I smiled around the strange company I'd somehow fallen into. "Order anything you like," I told them all firmly. "I know what I want—that kind of rolled-up bun that smells like cinnamon!"

It turned out to be called a cinnamon roll, which made sense, and it tasted even better than it smelled. Curled-up layers of pastry, sugar, and cinnamon melted into my tongue, and I relaxed more and more onto my cushion until I was actually following the goblins' lead and *sprawling* for the first time in my life. My deportment tutor would have been horrified—but I ignored every rule of behavior I'd ever learned as my companions' chatter washed happily over me.

The goblin girl with the peppermint sweet—the one who'd *hugged* me—was Talvikki. The prissy goblin girl, who took such nervous, proper care over everything, was Berrit. The third, who'd been in Villenne the longest and drawled every word as if she were exhausted, was Hannalena, and the kobold was Fedolia.

I absorbed every word and every name as if they were lessons I might be tested on at any moment—but I had *never* enjoyed my tutoring this much before.

"This can't be normal, can it?" I finally asked, as they argued over how many points Gert van Heidecker ought to be awarded for his personal resistance to the soldiers. "I mean, most university lectures aren't like that one, are they?"

Hannalena cocked one thick green eyebrow. "Only the really good ones."

I shook my head at her impatiently as the other girls sniggered. "But—Gert van Heidecker! He's so respected. He's certainly never published anything so—so—"

"Radical?" Berrit suggested helpfully.

"Treasonous?" muttered Jurgen.

Konrad nodded vigorously in agreement.

"I never read anything like that in his printed lectures," I said firmly to all of them.

"You think anyone would dare print lectures like that one?" Talvikki bumped one shoulder companionably against mine. "How naive are you, Sofi? They'd be in prison with him if they had!"

I'd adjusted so much by then, I barely even noticed the familiarity of her gesture, or the way I'd somehow acquired a nickname for the first time in my life. "So he's been saying these things for years?" How could I not have known that?

Hiding in my bedroom had kept me safe. But it had also kept me ignorant, and *that* was unacceptable.

"He wasn't always that fiery," Hannalena conceded. "He always had subversive tendencies, but he wasn't one of the real revolutionary firebrands—you know, the ones crying, 'Down with kings and monarchies forever!'"

She waved her fist and the other goblin girls gave mocking cheers. I swallowed uncomfortably, and my guards shifted behind me.

"But the Diamond Exhibition's really worked him up lately. It's not all farming tools and plans for new settlements in the icy north, you know. All those claims splashed about in the newspapers"—Hannalena flicked one wide green hand dismissively—"saying those fabulous new weapons are *sooo* undefeatable, they could even take down a dragon or an ice giant, much less any *human* uprisings—!"

"Ha!" Talvikki chomped down hard on her peppermint sweet. It cracked.

"Nothing could take down a dragon," I agreed.

"An ice giant could," Hannalena said flatly.

Studious Berrit narrowed her eyes in speculation. "Fedolia? What odds would you give a really big dragon in that fight? Say, if it was a really fierce one—"

"No odds," said Fedolia, and licked cinnamon-sugar off her glittering blue fingernails with her long, pointed tongue. A silver necklace hung around her neck, its bulky pendant hidden underneath her student robe, and she plucked at the chain absently with her free hand as she finished: "They wouldn't last two minutes."

"Is that a joke?" I stared at all of them, caught off-balance. Ice giants were only a problem in the far north, so

I'd never had to study them back home in Drachenheim—but even the magic-filled fairies of Elfenwald and a full army of human battle mages couldn't defeat a full-grown dragon. How could anything else ever do it?

"Oh, Sofi." Talvikki shook her head at me. "You do have an awful lot to learn. But don't worry . . ." She wrapped one protective arm around my shoulder. "You have us to show you around now! Aren't you glad?"

Behind me, Konrad let out a groan of horror.

Talvikki's sharp teeth shone in a startlingly sweet smile . . .

And I found myself smiling back at her with more ease than I'd felt in years.

"I can't wait," I said sincerely.

From: Sofia of Drachenheim
85 Svëavagen
The Cat's Room
Villenne

To: Jasper
The Hoard
The Cavern
Dragon Mountain

Dear Jasper,

You wouldn't believe everything I've seen since we arrived. I feel terrible that I haven't taken the time to write any of it down for you until now!

Somehow, I never seem to have any time for writing in the daytime anymore, and by the evenings I'm exhausted. I didn't even know I could walk so far in a day! If only you really could be here to explore with me. You would love it—and now that I'm not in the palace, there's no one to stop me going anywhere I like. Unfortunately, now that I'm trying to stay awake to write it out for you at last, the cat keeps walking all over my—

Oops.

Well, there's another smudge! So you can tell exactly what the cat's been up to, can't you?

(I'm sharing a room with a cat while I'm here. Lena and Anja think he must have been someone's pet once, because he is so friendly and so fond of petting. He's stray, but he's adopted me as his chief cuddler while we're here, which I understand is a great honor.)

I have explained to him that an open bottle of ink is not a stepping-stone, but he has very little common sense. Lena says cats rarely do.

(Anja says that's why she likes them. Ulrike only sniffed very loudly, to make it perfectly clear that she thinks I have no common sense, either.)

Right now, though, he is purring and butting his head against my chin, and he isn't likely to stop until I finally give in and lie down to cuddle him to sleep in the bed—and the truth is, I am tired.

But I hope that you're well! I'm sending you the latest volumes of Gert van Heidecker's lectures along with this letter. They arrived here a few days after we did, but I haven't had a chance to read them yet—and I doubt that I will for some time. So I'll let you have the pleasure of reading them first.

(And then I'll tell you all about his arrest! I was right there, watching it happen.)

Your friend,
Sofia

# CHAPTER 10

Ulrike might not have believed it, but apparently I did have some common sense left after all. As Talvikki nudged me toward the deep, sparkling seawater two weeks after we'd first met, I dug my feet into the rickety wooden jetty and resisted her with all my might. "I just don't think—"

"Oh, Sofi!" Letting go of me, she threw out her arms in exasperation. "Have you regretted *any* of our adventures so far?"

"Well . . ." In the past two weeks, I had followed her and the others down ancient, dripping goblin tunnels that no humans had ever seen before. We'd attended secret concerts of goblin music so eerie that listening to it had felt like discovering a whole new language. We'd attended lectures on new scientific and philosophical theories that had nearly made my head explode. Then we'd shouted over each other afterward in the underground coffeehouse, debating every one of our adventures, and I had loved every moment.

Still...

I peered over the wooden jetty that we shared—and shuddered as the thin planks creaked beneath me. Five more long, skinny wooden jetties stretched out across the water parallel to us, each of them spaced several feet apart. As I watched, the other goblin girls and Fedolia all walked happily down their own jetties, as if it was an ordinary, everyday activity to jump into deep, cold water without a qualm. Only my guards still stood on the forested beach of Villenne's least populated island, guarding our discarded student caps and looking intensely skeptical. Jurgen had already taken off his boots in obvious preparation for a rescue.

"The sea is *really deep*," I muttered to Talvikki. "And..." I *hated* admitting inadequacies. "I-don't-know-how-to-swim!" I mumbled.

"You don't need to!" She winked. "Just trust me, silly."

Incredibly, I did. That would have seemed unimaginable only three weeks ago, but the truth was, Talvikki had adopted me as her friend just as casually and inescapably as my new cat had acquired me as his person. I'd trained all my life to resist orders and fight against manipulation... but I was utterly helpless against easy, warm affection. I had never felt anything like it before.

"Why *are* you so nice to me?" The words tumbled out as I looked at Talvikki. I'd been holding them back for days, but something about this moment—wavering on the edge of the unfathomably deep Valmarene sea—tore them out of me against my will.

"Why shouldn't I be nice?" She frowned. "Was someone mean to you before we met? Do you want us to go and beat them up for you? We can do that, you know. All of us together—"

"No!" The idea of them charging on the Villennese palace was petrifying. "I only meant . . ."

Water sparkled all around us and the sun shone down on us as I sought for words and the other goblin girls chatted and laughed on their own wooden jetties. "You didn't have any humans in your group before me."

"Of course not." She shrugged. "But you're different, aren't you?"

"Oh." My stomach sank.

Of course I was different. I never really fit in anywhere, did I?

"That's not a *bad* thing, silly Sofi." She shook her head at me. "Haven't you noticed? There might be goblins and trolls and all manner of creatures sharing this city, but none of the humans ever look at any of us. They just stare straight past us like we don't even exist . . . except for you." She smiled. "*You've* been arguing with us ever since you first got here. Why wouldn't we want you for a friend?"

I let out a half laugh of disbelief. "You like me because I *argue* with you?"

Everyone I'd ever known had groaned and lectured me over my horrible temper. The whole curse of my life had been the fact that I could never let any argument go. But

Talvikki's grin stretched even wider at my words. "Of course! It's how we know you're being *honest* with us. You're treating us like we matter to you."

"Oh!" My eyes widened. "You *do* matter."

But I hadn't been honest with her about everything. All these days of shared adventures, all those arguments and jokes and dazzling new experiences . . . and still, as far as they all knew, I was a mere noblewoman, sent very young to the University of Villenne.

I took a deep breath, opened my mouth—and panic overwhelmed me. *No!*

Talvikki *liked* Sofi, the girl without any special expectations. That didn't mean she'd like Her Royal Highness Sofia of Drachenheim. No one else ever had after meeting me! I might just about manage as a *girl*, but as a princess I was an abject failure every time.

But I had to—I couldn't—

"Well?" said Talvikki. "Are you done worrying? You're going to love this, I promise. Just jump, and *then* you'll understand!"

My throat was too tight to let the truth about myself out . . . *ever.* But there was one thing I could do for her, at least.

"I trust you," I said, and jumped into the deep, cold Valmarene sea with my eyes wide open, as all the goblin girls whooped with joy and jumped in, too . . .

And then I landed on something hidden in the waves that sent me bouncing high into the air.

"Aaaah!"

It was a trampoline—an invisible trampoline!

"It's silver mesh!" Talvikki shouted gleefully as she bounced beside me. "Woven so fine you can't even see it! Didn't I tell you you would love it?"

*Love* it? I was flying! I didn't even need a dragon! I landed back on the transparent mesh and took off even higher, flinging my arms out in midair and whooping with joy for the first time in my life.

"It's like magic!"

"Even better!" Berrit called from her own net. "It's *cleverness!*" With a determined look in her eyes, she executed a perfect flip, her blue student robes flying around her green head.

Talvikki grabbed my hands. "Let's try that together!" she said. "One, two . . . three!"

We landed on the mesh a moment later in a hopeless tangle of student robes and arms, laughing uncontrollably. As Talvikki leaped up to her feet, I lay back on the net, letting salty, cold seawater soak through the fine mesh into the back of my hair and robe as the net swung and bounced irrepressibly beneath me.

The sky spread wide and blue and full of possibility. Laughter and friendship surrounded me.

I'd do anything to keep this feeling. *Anything.*

But when I rolled back to my feet on the wildly bouncing net, I found the small blue-and-white kobold, Fedolia, watching me from her own net with narrowed ice-chip eyes . . . and with unmistakable suspicion written all over her face.

\* \* \*

It wasn't hard to walk apart from Fedolia on our way back to the main islands. Once I thought about it, I realized she had never voluntarily come close to me in the last two weeks. The goblin girls were all so loud and friendly, I'd barely noticed her coolness before—but now that I was watching, I could see it all too clearly.

With the others, she was sharp and glittery and fun, full of smirking comments and bright laughter, but her eyes flicked past me every time, and her face tightened whenever I stepped too close. No matter how many times I tried to catch her gaze as we left the trampolines behind, she never, ever looked at me.

It made my stomach crawl with discomfort. Did she just not like me—or humans in general? Or did she suspect I wasn't being honest after all?

I dropped behind the rest of the dripping, cheerful group and tugged Talvikki back with me. "Is there a reason Fedolia doesn't like me?" I whispered.

"Fedolia?" Talvikki's thick eyebrows shot up as her steps slowed. "I'm sure she likes you."

"No, she doesn't," I said firmly. "Trust me." I had *plenty* of practice dealing with people who didn't like me but were forced to deal with me because of my family. I knew exactly how forced acceptance felt.

"Well, it can't be anything too bad, can it?" She shrugged. "I wouldn't take it personally. She's just . . . a kobold. There's no one else like her in this whole city, you know?"

I frowned. "I've seen other kobolds in the coffeehouse."

"But have you ever seen any of them talk to our Fedolia?"

Talvikki shook her head. "I know she can be moody—and she's fond of tricks and pranks, like most kobolds are—but she has good reasons for not trusting easily, after the way her people cast her out."

"What?" I came to a halt as we reached the trail that led through the woods toward civilization, holding her back with me. "What do you mean they cast her out?"

Talvikki shot a quick look up ahead, then dropped her voice as she leaned closer to murmur in my ear. "You know how we all come from up north? Well, none of us *wanted* to leave our home in the first place. A few years ago, though, a goblin family accidentally tunneled too close to the ice giants' hidden treasures. It turned into a total disaster for all of us. That whole family was taken prisoner—even the babies! Can you believe it? Then the giants kicked out all the rest of us. Only the kobolds were allowed to stay in their territory, and *they* had to agree to be the giants' spies, to make sure everybody else keeps out from now on."

She sighed. "That's why those famous Diamond Exhibition machines and expansion plans are so ridiculous! Any goblin could tell King Henrik: the ice giants won't allow anyone else to share their realm anymore."

Talking about realms made me remember being a princess, which was the last thing I wanted right now. "What happened to Fedolia?"

"She didn't obey." Talvikki's face creased with sadness. "She used her invisibility trick to help that family of prisoners escape. She has a kind heart under all that glitter—but the giants somehow found out that she was the one who'd done it."

"Oh no." My eyes widened. "What happened?"

"I have no idea how she got away without being frozen herself—*or* executed." Talvikki shrugged. "She won't talk about it, *ever*. But I do know she's never allowed to go home again . . . and not one of the other kobolds in town will even look at her. *They're* all loyal to the ice giants even now, for the sake of keeping their families safe back home—and Fedolia's own family cut her off completely to save themselves."

*Ohhh.* I shook my head as we fell into step behind the others.

There was so much about the world outside my palace that I still didn't understand. Apparently, though, I wasn't the only one who'd been scooped up just when I needed it most by this extraordinary group of friends here in Villenne. Fedolia had been, too.

Could *that* explain why she was so suspicious of me? Maybe she thought I was trying to take her place in the group.

If only she knew, she had nothing to worry about. A few weeks from now, I'd have to drag myself home to face my own punishment, leaving all this joyous freedom behind forever.

But I wouldn't let anyone—not even a mysterious, magical kobold—stop me from savoring every moment until then.

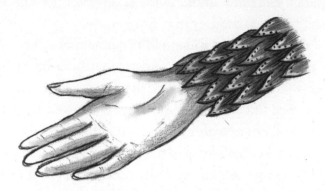

# CHAPTER 11

"... So then we'll go to Knights' Island for lemon ices this afternoon, and do some shopping before we come home," Anja finished happily. She sat perched on a chair beside me while my maid smoothed cream and a comb through my thick, long hair—which was only now starting to recover from yesterday's seawater immersion—and Lena fussed around me, checking every finicky detail of my striped blue-and-lavender gown.

It was really one of Anja's gowns, of course; I'd borrowed them every day for the past two weeks, and the two cousins accompanied each new gown every morning to chat on and on at me about the day ahead, just as they and Ulrike had done every day back in Drachenburg.

Ulrike didn't come with them anymore, thank goodness.

I'd ordered her not to write to my sister about anything that I was doing, and she'd grumpily agreed—but now she spent her mornings sulking in her parlor downstairs, making certain I knew how much she disapproved of every choice I'd made ever since we'd arrived. Anja and Lena, on the other hand, were giddy with freedom—from the proper royal court, from their duties, and, for most of each day, from me—and it had made me realize that I wasn't the only one who had felt trapped back at home.

Perhaps that was why, for the first time since they'd been foisted on me two years ago, I didn't find it annoying at all to let their birdlike chatter wash over me each morning as I was dressed.

"I saw some *lovely* new fans on Knights' Island!" Lena said as she tucked a final pleat on my borrowed gown into place. "I want a light pink one to match my best gown *and* a bright yellow one for the summer months. And of course, we *could* pick up an extra fan for you, too, Your Highness, if you wanted . . . er?" She darted a wary look around my shoulder, as if I might erupt at her in a temper for her suggestion.

"No, thank you," I said politely. I couldn't think of anything in the world that sounded less interesting to acquire, but I forced a semi-gracious nod to reassure her.

Lena gave me a tiny half smile in return.

Anja bounced off her chair. "Are you *finally* ready, Lena? I want to watch the parade of the horse guards! It's almost time for them to start."

"Just a moment." Lena hesitated a few feet away from me, her expression softer and more open than I'd ever seen before. "What are your own plans for today, Your Highness? If you don't mind me asking, I mean."

"Oh, I don't know everything I'll do!" I couldn't even help the smile that spread across my face as I considered it. "There are two different lectures I *might* attend, but I'm meeting Talvikki and the others at a coffeehouse first, so . . . we'll see! They always have ideas of their own."

Of course, I'd never told my ladies-in-waiting any of the details of *those* adventures. I didn't dare even hint that Talvikki and the others weren't actually human. Apart from our sinister Elfenwald invaders six months ago, no non-humans had ever openly walked the streets of Drachenburg. Our dragon allies only flew overhead once a week, and our people had *still* gone into conniptions over the danger before they'd finally adjusted to our groundbreaking new alliance.

If proper Ulrike ever discovered that I was consorting with goblins, she would fall over in a swoon of horror—and then bundle me into a carriage headed straight to Drachenburg for my own safety.

*That* was why I'd forced my guards to promise never to tell her, on threat of slipping outside without them and putting myself in even more danger next time. I'd told my ladies-in-waiting only that I'd made friends on Scholars' Island—and, after all, that was completely true. If you looked at it from just the right angle, I wasn't *lying* to them any more than I was "lying" to my friends. I was simply . . . keeping back some irrelevant truths from each of them, to make sure that both parts of my Villennese life stayed totally and completely separate.

So the knock on the front door of our house, five minutes later, came as a stomach-churning surprise.

No one was supposed to know I lived here! I'd never told Talvikki and the others my address.

Oh no. What if the awful king and queen of Valmarna had actually decided to *forgive* me? That could be their messenger *right now*, coming to bring me back to join the other royals at the palace.

I had to get rid of him before Ulrike found out!

At least a quarter of my long cloud of thick black curls was still hanging down my back, un-combed, un-pinned, and hopelessly out of place. I lunged out of my maid's hands anyway and flung the door open without waiting for her to do it. Thank goodness Anja's skirts weren't quite as long or as heavy as mine! Gathering them up in both hands, I hurtled down the creaking staircase so quickly that I sounded like a herd of wild horses stampeding through the house.

Ulrike's voice floated up the stairs. "Show him into my parlor, if you please."

*Him?* None of my goblin friends were boys . . . so it really had to be the royal messenger. *Disaster!* Ulrike would accept that invitation on my behalf while weeping tears of joy. We'd be packed before I could say a word in protest!

There had to be something I could do to stop myself being bundled away against my will again. I couldn't lose my friends already!

*Aha.* A perfect plan roared through me.

Last time, I hadn't even meant to get myself uninvited from the palace. This time, I was ready.

I yanked out all the pins from my hair. They scattered and showered down the narrow staircase. *Much better!* I rolled up my sleeves like a yokel as my hair burst out in a gorgeously untamed cloud around me. Then I set my face into an intimidating scowl, and stomped the rest of the way down to Ulrike's parlor, prepared to be a diplomat's *worst nightmare*.

Ulrike jumped as I slammed the door open with a *thunk!* that sent it crashing against the flowered wallpaper. The dark-haired boy who stood facing her, though, didn't shift so much as an inch. Did he have nerves of steel, to ignore a sound like that?

He wasn't wearing noble dress, or a typical messenger's uniform, either. Instead of a jacket and trousers, he wore a bizarre, one-piece cloth outfit patterned with what looked almost like . . . *scales?*

Yes! Those curving purple-and-blue repeated shapes were actually intended to look like *dragon scales*, all across his arms and legs and back. *What in the world?*

The Valmarene royals didn't even like dragons! If that snooty king and queen thought they could get away with using *our* allies' scales in *their* messengers' uniforms—!

Scowling ferociously, I stalked forward to let him know exactly what I thought of him *and* his rulers, too.

"Your Highness!" Ulrike stared at my bare forearms and unpinned hair in horror.

"*Highness?*" The boy spun around with a dazzling white smile.

I stopped, rocking backward as that smile hit me.

He should have looked awkward in his outlandish outfit.

Instead, he looked *right*, in a way that had me tugging my own sleeves back into place as I stared at him, speechlessly taking in his wide, infectious grin, his thick black hair, his pale skin, his long legs, and his strangely familiar golden eyes . . .

*Wait.*

Humans didn't have golden eyes.

Every dragon I'd ever met had had them, though . . . including Jasper's aunt, Émeraude, who'd carried us to Villenne . . . and Jasper's dark-haired sister, Aventurine, a magical dragon-girl chocolatier and food mage who could *shift back and forth between shapes on command.*

"Uhhh . . . ihhhh . . . !"

I slammed my lips shut too late. My feet backed hastily toward the door.

But he was already hurrying toward me, his face alight with excitement. "Sofia?" he said eagerly. "Is it you? You look *exactly* like I'd always imagined!"

*Nonononono!*

I was suddenly, paralyzingly aware of two excruciating truths at once:

I looked like an absolute disaster . . . and if I didn't get hold of myself *immediately*, I was about to faint for the first time in my life, in front of the one person in the world I most wanted to like me.

I was a *princess.* The honor of Drachenheim was at stake!

So I called on all my years of royal training, stiffened every muscle to force myself upright, and said in a voice like a frog's croak of terror:

"I am so glad to finally meet you in person . . . Jasper!"

# CHAPTER 12

"I decided to leave the moment I read your letter," Jasper told me ten minutes later.

We were sitting together on a faded sofa in my own private parlor upstairs, but of course Ulrike had insisted on accompanying us. How else could she spy on everything we said or did and pass every detail on to my sister?

Luckily, Jasper didn't seem to notice her nosiness. All his attention was divided between me and the enormous pile of pastries that he was devouring at an unbelievable rate. His body might have changed from dragon to human, but his appetite certainly hadn't adjusted to the shift.

"How could I not follow your example?" He scarfed down a fifth large cinnamon roll and reached for a sixth with his free hand. "My aunt told us all about how brave you were, throwing yourself out of your carriage in mid-air just to tell all those soldiers what you thought of them!"

"Um . . ." I darted a nervous glance at Ulrike, who dropped her own gaze swiftly back to her embroidery. "That's . . . not exactly the way it happened, but—"

"Don't you remember what you wrote in your letter? '*If only you really could be here to explore with me.*'" He beamed. "Now I am! And just think: we can go meet Gert van Heidecker *in person.*"

"Well . . ." I forced myself not to look at Ulrike. "That part might not be as easy as you'd think." Needless to say, my senior lady-in-waiting had *not* been informed of my favorite philosopher's arrest, so I couldn't explain the facts of human prisons to Jasper in front of her. "There are plenty of other things we *can* do," I said hastily. "But first . . ."

I gestured helplessly from his tousled black hair to his booted feet. "How did this happen?" All-too-conscious of Ulrike listening in, I dropped my voice to a whisper. "Are you a food mage, too, like your sister?"

"Me? Ha!" He swallowed down a long sip of spiced apple tea. "She'd laugh to hear you say that. Aventurine always said, though, that she'd help me change if I ever wanted to. So, when I read your letter, I knew it was time to make her finally keep her promise. She was visiting the cave, so it was easy to manage the spell while the others slept. I can shift back and forth as much as I want to, now, just like her! So I flew all the way until I reached Villenne and then shifted shape just outside the city."

No wonder he was hungry! "That's a *long* first flight." I pushed the nearly empty plate closer to him.

"Aventurine told me I'd never make it all the way here on my own. *She* thought I'd turn tail and fly back to the cave and all my books the first moment my wings grew tired." His grin deepened into a smirk. "I *told* her she was wrong."

*Aha!* I smirked back at him, suddenly comfortable after all, despite the shock of his unexpected visit *and* the awkwardness of Ulrike eavesdropping on every word. I might never have dared to meet him in real life, but now that I had . . .

"Just wait," I told him. "Drachenburg is tiny compared to Villenne. You'll see things Aventurine has never even heard of! And," I finished with deep satisfaction, "I can show you everything myself."

The sound of Ulrike's anguished sigh was music to my ears.

We set off half an hour later, once my hair was finally combed and pinned and I'd dealt with the last of Ulrike's squawking protests. I wore my student robes over Anja's striped gown; Jasper went as he was in his scale-patterned outfit and a pair of far-too-big battered brown boots that he'd found abandoned on a street corner. Luckily, he didn't seem to notice the curious glances his clothing garnered from everyone we passed on our way to Scholars' Island. He was too busy swinging his head from side to side, asking question after question without a break.

"So that's a house? And that's one, too, even though it looks so different? And—oh, *that's* a lamppost? I never imagined them looking like that!"

I'd spent the last nine months terrified of letting Jasper discover my true flaws, in case he decided to end our friendship over any of them. I'd been certain that if we ever met, I'd be awkward and disastrous and he would give up on me immediately.

But this? This was easy. This was actually *fun!*

"I can't wait to introduce you to the others," I told him as I stepped onto the crowded white student bridge. I'd lost all my graceful deportment days ago. Now I strode forward with my elbows stuck out to clear my way through the constant, jostling crowd. I was already peering ahead in search of the ever-shifting table that sold secondhand student robes like mine.

Jurgen tapped me on the shoulder. "My lady?"

I turned around—and groaned. We'd left Jasper behind! I shoved my way back through the crowd to find him still standing, staring, before the bridge. His golden eyes widened more and more as people shoved past him from both directions.

"There are so . . . *many* . . ."

*Ohhh.* "I understand," I told him. And I did.

That first time I'd stepped out of our borrowed house had been awful. How much worse would it be for someone who'd spent his entire life in a cavern beneath a mountain, with no one around him but his own family?

Jasper wasn't just funny and clever and kind—he was *so* brave to come flying into the unknown. Unlike me, he hadn't even needed anyone else to force him into it.

I couldn't let him stumble now.

So I took a deep breath, reached out and tucked my right hand securely under Jasper's arm, the way I'd seen Anja and Lena do for each other when one of them was sagging with tiredness or nerves.

"Come on." I tugged him gently forward. "Don't let yourself think about any of those strangers around us."

"Don't *think*—?" His dark eyebrows rose skeptically. His pale throat bobbed with a nervous swallow.

"Think about this instead," I said firmly. "At Gert van Heidecker's lecture, he asked us all to consider the definition of true power."

Jasper let out a snorting laugh and took a slow step forward. Jurgen stepped wordlessly into place on his other side, shielding him, as Jasper said, "If you ask anyone in my family, they'll tell you *flame and claws*. But from a human point of view, I suppose . . ."

Konrad let out a soft moan behind me. Had no one bothered to fill him in on Jasper's background? Never mind. We were all learning new things in Villenne.

I kept my gaze on Jasper's drawn face, forcing him to hold my gaze as we moved forward.

"Humans are obsessed with blood, aren't you?" said Jasper. "So—"

"What? *No!*" I wrinkled my nose in disgust. "Don't be ridiculous! You're the ones who eat raw meat! We don't—"

"Blood*lines*, I meant. That's what you call them, isn't it?" He waved one long-fingered hand impatiently, his stride lengthening as his brows lowered in concentration. "I'm always reading about it in your books—everyone worrying endlessly over who was born to whom, as if *that* should decide how important they were, instead of anything about their own strengths."

*That* struck far too close to home after everything Van Heidecker had said about royalty in his lecture. I scowled up at Jasper, forgetting all about reassurance. "Don't tell me dragons don't care who's born to whom! Your family would do anything for their hatchlings. They're only protecting Drachenburg because your sister lives there."

"That's *entirely* different," he said. "Dragons always protect their territory—including their own families, of course. But they don't expect anyone else to think their hatchlings are more important than—"

"Ahem." Jurgen coughed politely. "My lady? You were intending to buy a student robe for your visitor?"

*Oops.* We'd come to the end of the bridge without realizing it! I grimaced and spun around to forge my way back through the chaos.

This time, Jasper didn't need urging to follow. We argued all the way back to the sales table, and his voice was only slightly muffled by the long blue robe that slipped over his head a minute later. As its folds slid down to cover his scale-patterned outfit, his face emerged, words still flowing without a break.

". . . If you consider the idea of power as an *illusion*—"

"I wouldn't call a ten-thousand-strong army an *illusion*," I retorted as Jurgen paid the saleswoman. "Unless you think you can close your eyes and imagine—"

"*Make way!*"

It took a lot to break through the cheerful chaos of students and salespeople mingling together, but at that sudden, deep-throated bellow, I jumped aside along with everybody else around me. A torrent of small figures thundered past us down the center of the bridge. Their green heads tucked against their chests for speed, and their feet pounded hard against the ancient white stone as they fled Scholars' Island in a panicked stream.

"Those aren't humans!" said Jasper. "Are they—?"

"Goblins," I confirmed unhappily.

As the final goblin disappeared into the crowded street beyond, every human left behind stared after them in a moment of stunned silence. Then life settled back to normal all around me as everyone turned away with nervous laughs and shakes of their heads, shrugging it off like any other odd city incident.

I couldn't shake it off so easily. I'd recognized nearly all those goblins from my trips to their secret coffeehouse beneath the library . . . which was exactly where I was heading right now.

Had the university finally discovered it? If they'd sent guards to shut it down . . .

I *couldn't* walk into another raid! I'd barely escaped the last one.

. . . But I hadn't seen any of my friends in that group.

What if they hadn't gotten out in time? What if they *needed* me?

A moan of indecision worked its way up my throat—and then a strong hand grabbed my arm.

"*There* you are, Sofi!" Talvikki popped into view beside me, making Jasper give a violent startle.

Fedolia must have been casting invisibility over all of them beforehand. All three goblin girls stood close around me now, while Fedolia stood behind them, carefully brushing off her blue robe with her long, white fingers while her silver necklace glinted around her neck in the bright sunlight. My shoulders slumped with relief, but a low, dangerous growl rumbled up from Jasper's throat.

His teeth were bared, lips pulling back in an inhuman snarl as he shouldered forward as if to shield me. Suddenly my sweet, funny, intellectual friend looked as wild as any of his relatives—and far less safe than I'd imagined.

"It's all right!" I said hastily. I didn't touch him this time, but I shifted between him and Talvikki. "They're my friends. I couldn't tell you all the details in front of Ulrike, but—"

"He's a friend of yours, too, eh?" Talvikki leaned around me, eyes bright, and took a fearless sniff of Jasper's robe. "He doesn't *smell* human." She shrugged. "Smells like cinnamon rolls, though. Apple tea, too."

Fedolia smacked her blue lips as she held up her fingers, carefully inspecting her glittering blue nails without sparing me a single glance. "Mm, apple tea."

"Ooh." Berrit gave a wistful sigh. "*I'd* like some apple tea right now. Not a cinnamon roll, though. Not today. Maybe a slice of fresh apple cake, or—"

"We have to go." There was no sign of Hannalena's usual cynical amusement as she cast a quick, sharp glance around the horizon. "We were just looking for you, Sofi, to warn you before we left. You need to leave Villenne, too, as quickly as possible. Go anywhere you want—but make sure it's far away from here. And don't stop to pack!"

"What are you talking about?" I shook my head in disbelief. "Why would you all leave the city? And *today*? We had plans!"

"Plans change." She nodded to the others. "Come on."

"Wait!" I grabbed Talvikki's robed arm, holding her back. "Tell me what's happening!"

Grimacing, she glanced between me and the other girls as they started down the bridge without her. "You remember that troll who was sleeping in the coffeehouse?"

I blinked. "The one who's been asleep for thirty years?"

"He's wide awake now," she said grimly, "because he felt it through the earth: *bad visitors coming.* He told all of us: *get out fast.*"

"But—"

"Trust me: after everything we went through up north? We don't stand around and wait when we get those warnings." She sighed. "I'll miss you, though, Sofi. Keep on having adventures, won't you? Maybe I'll see you again one day."

She pulled free with one quick twitch. Less than a minute later, she had vanished with the others into the swirling crowd of blue robes, leaving me staring helplessly after them.

The sun still shone overhead. Sparkling blue water rippled beyond the bridge. Students and salesmen argued and laughed around me as if nothing had changed.

"Do you think I did this?" Jasper asked hesitantly. "If that troll sensed me flying toward the city and got spooked—"

A scream sounded just in front of us.

Another scream ripped through the air. Then another and another, until almost everyone on the bridge was pointing in our direction and screaming with one panicked voice:

"DRAGON!"

"What?" I sucked in my breath as my guards leaped to flank me. *It's not possible.* Those strangers couldn't have figured out Jasper's secret! He hadn't changed shape, or—

"Oh no," Jasper breathed. He was staring behind me, too.

I turned to follow his horrified gaze . . . and my heart sank. "Oh *no*."

The unmistakable silhouette of an enormous dragon flapped inexorably toward us. From its claws dangled a carriage with a flag hanging from it.

A perfectly, horribly familiar flag.

"That's my mother!" Jasper's voice sounded half-strangled.

"Worse yet," I whispered. "I'm almost certain that's my *sister.*"

We were both in *so much* trouble.

CHAPTER 13

The journey back to my borrowed house went much too quickly. Jasper didn't ask any questions about our surroundings, and I didn't distract him with philosophy. We just hurried in horrible, grim silence as the wide streets of Villenne emptied around us, everyone scrambling for cover.

The Villennese royal guards were waiting outside my front step when we arrived.

"Your Highness." The captain of the guard jerked a bow, his sword gleaming by his side. "If you'll allow us to escort you to the palace . . ."

"Of course." I sighed. "Just let me change my clothes, and then—"

"I'm afraid that won't be possible." His gaze flicked across my blue student robes and then snapped back to my face. "Their Majesties instructed me to escort you to them without delay."

"But—"

"Without *any* delay," he said firmly.

My guards stiffened behind me, but I sagged in defeat. "Oh, fine," I mumbled.

*Of course* I would be dressed like a commoner when I greeted my sister in front of the sneering local royals. How else could this day get even worse?

"Your Highness!" Ulrike rushed out of the house, her pale hands twisting together before her chest. "Oh, thank goodness they've found you. I've been so worried—"

"Have you, Ulrike? Have you, really?" I swung around, letting panic transform into righteous fury. "Didn't I *specifically* order you not to write to my sister? How *dare* you—"

"I didn't!" Her voice came out as a gasp. "I would never disobey a direct order, Your Highness, no matter how deeply I disapproved. You must know that!"

"Then how do you explain *my sister* flying all the way out here to—"

"Ahem." Jurgen cleared his throat beside me.

My head whipped around. "*You?*"

"Forgive me, Your Highness," he rumbled quietly. "But your safety was my first concern. I'd made a commitment to the crown princess, you see, before we left."

. . . And my sister was right. I *was* a fool!

I'd ordered him not to tell *Ulrike* what I was doing—but I should have known that my ladies-in-waiting weren't the only ones spying on me for my sister. When I thought of everywhere my guards had accompanied me over the past two and a half weeks—everywhere that Katrin would soon know I'd gone, if she didn't already . . . !

Nausea roiled through me in a sickening rush. I staggered and doubled over, struggling to catch my breath.

"Sofia?" Jasper grabbed my arm, his voice rising. "Are you ill? Do you have some sort of strange human *disease*?"

"Not yet." I gritted my teeth into the rictus of a smile and forced myself upright into perfect-princess-posture. "I'm just . . . preparing myself for the boat trip ahead."

"We'll go faster by carriage," the captain told me.

". . . Of course we will." A bitter laugh tore itself from my throat. That whole dreadful, endless boat ride when we'd first arrived—! I should have known the queen of Valmarna was having fun at my expense.

She would get plenty more entertainment from me and my family soon enough.

I marched into the Valmarene royal carriage with my back as stiff as any of the wooden boards I'd been strapped to as a toddler to train for days like today, when I would need to stand tall while the whole world watched, no matter how shattered I felt inside.

As my guards and Ulrike settled into place nearby, I stared sightlessly out the closest window, refusing to meet any of their gazes. Even when I heard Jasper settle himself into the seat across from me, I didn't let myself turn to face him.

I was a princess of Drachenheim. I would not let anyone glimpse tears in my eyes.

They were gone by the time we reached the central

island where the royal palace sprawled, only twenty minutes later. I held myself rigid with determination, my jaw locking as I watched those glorious white walls curve into view.

*Just endure this until it's over,* I told myself.

Humiliation had never killed anyone before. For better or worse, it wouldn't kill me now, either.

Gert van Heidecker would say—

No. I wouldn't think about him right now. I couldn't let myself think about anyone I'd seen or met since my arrival, because if I did, I would break down entirely.

*"Maybe I'll see you again one day . . ."*

If I'd ever been brave enough to tell Talvikki the truth of who I was, she would have known better than to imagine that that could ever happen. But I hadn't—I'd been too cowardly—so she and the others would never know who it really was that they'd welcomed into their group for one magical moment.

The carriage pulled to a halt. The door swung open. "Your Highness." The captain of the Valmarene guard stood outside, waiting for me.

I walked down the carriage steps with my head held high, my long, blue secondhand student robe swishing around me. Jasper must have scrambled after me; I sensed him walking behind me a moment later. His quick, unsteady breaths sounded uncomfortably loud in my ears.

But all my attention was fixed on the scene spread out before me, like a perfectly staged reenactment of my arrival at Villenne weeks ago.

Rows of soldiers and black-cloaked battle mages filled the

massive, checkered square. The sea glittered, blue and vast, surrounding us on three sides, while the palace sprawled on the fourth side, closing all of us in together. Sunlight shot sparks off the rippling water.

In the center of it all stood the king and queen of Valmarna ... but this time, they weren't alone. *No such luck.* They were flanked by two half circles of men, women, and girls and boys around my own age, all of them wearing elaborate gowns and jackets—and Ulrike had been right: I *could* tell the difference between the outfit of a lady-in-waiting and a royal after all, even before I started recognizing faces from public portraits.

I was looking at the assembled royalty of the continent. While I'd been gallivanting around the city with my friends, they had all gathered together for the Diamond Exhibition ... so they were *all* here now to witness my disgrace.

*Everyone* would see what was about to happen.

I felt as if I was floating above my body as I watched my sister's carriage descend through the air. The shadow of Jasper's mother's great wings cast cool darkness across the checkered square. I didn't move as the shadow fell over me. I was helpless to do anything except stand and take what was coming to me.

I was always so helpless when I was myself, undisguised. And I was so, so very tired of it.

At least Katrin would never unleash her fury in front of everyone. She was far too conscious of her dignity and our nation's reputation to ever berate me in front of onlookers.

The carriage landed with a *thump* directly in front of me. Above it, Jasper's mother opened her vast mouth wide in a soundless roar, her ferocious golden eyes fixed on her runaway son. I heard Jasper gulp. My own dread-filled gaze fixed on the carriage door as it fell open . . .

And my sister tumbled out of it, barely catching herself on the doorframe as she tripped. My mouth fell open as I stared at her.

Katrin was barely recognizable! From the tangled, messy knots of dark hair that hung around my sister's beautiful light brown face to the haggard look on her face as she staggered painfully down the carriage steps . . .

Apparently, we did have something in common after all, because I could actually smell the sick from here.

Cringing in sympathy, I started forward.

Queen Berghild spoke before I could. "So! Yet again, another Drachenheim . . . *princess* . . ." She paused on the word, as she glanced from my disheveled sister to the other, elegant watching royals. ". . . Has terrified our citizens for no reason, without giving us the benefit of a fair warning. Princess Katrin, I'm not surprised after all that you could only find *wild beasts* to ally with your little kingdom."

Grinding my teeth, I swung on her. A terrifying growl rolled through the courtyard, stopping me in my tracks.

But it wasn't Jasper's mother who had made that ominous sound. It was my elegant, perfectly controlled older sister who had shockingly let it loose . . .

. . . As she glared directly at me. "Do you have *any idea what you've put me through, Sofia?*" She didn't even seem to notice the queen of Valmarna, or any of the other gathered royals who were all avidly watching us.

"Katrin!" I jerked my head urgently toward our audience. "We can't—"

"*Three days!*" she shouted into my face. "Three whole *days* of endless sickness!"

"I *know*," I gritted through my teeth. "I did it, too! But—"

"I had to leave the kingdom under *Father's* control," she spat. "Do you have any idea what the nobles will talk him into while I'm gone? Do you even *care* that our most vulnerable subjects will suffer for it?"

"I—"

"Of course you don't! You don't care about any of us!" She swept out one arm, nearly falling over with the force of her gesture. Two of her senior ladies-in-waiting hovered behind her, peering out the carriage doorway with identically terrified expressions. No *one* had ever seen her lose control before today. "You certainly don't care about me!" she bellowed.

"Katrin—"

"I asked you to do *one thing*, Sofia. *One!* How hard could it be, for once in your life, to actually *help* our kingdom instead of feeding off it?"

*Ouch.* I sucked in my breath as our onlookers rustled with interest. I had to control my expression for my own sake *and* for our kingdom, no matter what she said. But . . .

"Why can't you even *pretend* to care that you're a princess?" Katrin demanded.

*That. Was. It!* Gasps hissed through the teeth of every nearby royal, and fury detonated within me.

Every day of my life that I'd spent pretending to be someone I wasn't, just to follow those stupid rules of royalty; *every day* that I'd worked to impress my sister while knowing I would *never* be good enough for her; every dream I'd given up because *a princess could never do that*; and everyone I would *never see again* after today—

"I don't know!" I shouted back. "Why don't you tell me? Because *you're* the one embarrassing our kingdom right now in front of everyone!"

Katrin jerked back as if she had been slapped. Her dark eyes flared wide. Her head snapped around . . .

And she finally noticed our gathered audience of royals.

Her face tightened with horror. Her long throat moved in a convulsive swallow as she looked from one disapproving face to another.

Then her eyes fastened on me with a light I'd never seen before, not even in the worst of our past arguments. "This," she hissed, "is *your fault*, Sofia. And I will never, *ever* forgive you for it."

# CHAPTER 14

The sea still lapped at the edges of the square, barely five meters from my feet. Seagulls still called to each other in the distance.

But inside me, an entire revolution took place, flushing me hot and cold until even the tips of my fingers tingled with the shock of it . . . and the realization:

How long had I been waiting for her to say those words to me?

All those years she'd spent dutifully looking after me, ever since our mother had died and Father had lost all real interest in us . . .

I'd always known that Katrin would give up on me one day, too. I'd just never expected her to do it in public, without even the pretense that she cared.

My eyes blurred. Something hot and fierce sparked behind them—and I realized: I couldn't hold back these tears after all, no matter how many people were watching.

"*Now*," said Katrin, swishing past me. "Your Majesties . . ."

I didn't wait to hear which beautifully polished words she would use to apologize for my behavior and excuse her own. Everyone here knew already that I had been discarded. What was the point of staying to hear more?

At least my legs still worked. They turned me around like a puppet and took off, half running, half stumbling down the square.

"Sofia!" Jasper called after me.

"Your Highness!" Ulrike cried. "Wait!"

"*Jasper!*" His mother's thunderous voice roared overhead. "*Don't you dare run away again!*"

Footsteps thudded after me as I dodged, running faster and faster, past rows of Villennese guards and battle mages who leaped out of my way. My long robe and gown tangled with my legs, so I yanked them up to my knees. It wasn't as if I could look any *less* regal at this point.

All that mattered was getting away from everyone . . . especially the only family I'd had left.

"I *will never, ever forgive you.*"

A harsh noise caught in my throat, somewhere between a sob and a croak.

Then a deafening mass of sound suddenly erupted behind me. Salt water crashed over the entire square in an overwhelming, icy wave. Dripping and spluttering, I spun around . . .

... And screamed as I saw three pairs of massive white hands, each one larger than my entire body, clenching around the three sea-facing sides of the big, tiled square. Ice shot out from boulder-sized fingertips, transforming every ounce of seawater that had puddled on the tiles and sending all of us helplessly staggering and skidding. Battle mages and soldiers looked tiny in comparison as they stumbled and slid, shouting, toward those three huge pairs of hands.

And beyond them, rising higher and higher ...

A strangled squeak escaped my lips as I tilted my head back to take in the full scope of the three monstrous figures emerging from their hiding places in the deep, cold seawater.

Long, dangling white beards hung down their bodies, tangled with shards of jagged ice. Marbled blue-and-white skin stretched higher than the palace walls. Massive eyes glared down upon us all like bright blue flames.

"Ice giants," I whispered.

They had to be.

They must have crawled on hands and knees between the islands all the way here, to keep from being witnessed until it was too late.

No wonder that troll had woken up at the underground echo of their movements. It hadn't been Jasper's mother who had spooked him after all.

She wheeled around now in midair, letting out a roar of fury that shook through my bones. Flame shot from her vast mouth as she flew at them, her giant teeth and claws stretching toward the ice giant in the center ...

... And he grabbed her by her long, scaly neck, closing

his massive fingers around it. Her dragonfire cut off in an instant.

Battle mages chanted in unison. Guards fired muskets. But white frost crackled and shot across her blue-and-gold scales—and an instant later, a tight, cold cage of ice encased her.

Her huge legs and wings stopped moving. Her great, golden eyes stared unseeing out from her transparent prison as the giant gathered it into his arms, hefting the giant block of ice with ease.

"*Mother!*" Jasper roared. He'd been standing just before me, but now he ran, skidding and sliding across the icy square, desperately fighting his way through the chaos toward the massive ice giant who held his mother.

A wordless moan of protest ripped out of my mouth as I reached uselessly after him. That creature had just defeated a full-grown dragon without a flinch! What could *he* possibly do against it? The battle mages' spells flickered and flashed in the air, bouncing off all three giants without any effect. Bullets and cannonballs landed on blue-and-white skin, but none of them left a single mark.

We had to run as fast as we could in the opposite direction, just as my other friends had told me! But Jasper ran straight at danger as I watched—and then something even worse happened.

My sister stepped forward. She held up one slim brown hand to forestall anyone from shielding her. "Now, gentlemen," she called up to the ice giants, in the firm but patient tone I'd heard her use on arrogant nobles many times before. "There is no need for any of this violence."

Without so much as glancing backward, she flicked one dismissive hand behind her at the square-full of battle mages and soldiers, and—perhaps simply in surprise—they all stepped back at once, leaving the courtyard in a sudden, stunned silence. Even Jasper stopped moving. From royals to guards, everyone gaped at my sister as the spells disappeared and the muskets and cannons stopped firing. Even the three ice giants looked surprised as they shifted together to stare down at her.

Only I wasn't shocked. Of course Katrin was handling it. Katrin handled everything! Unlike me, she was a true princess.

But my feet stayed stubbornly planted on the ground nonetheless, refusing to turn away until I actually *saw* her make everyone safe . . .

. . . Especially herself. Because as those three ice giants shifted to loom together over my sister, my stomach curled up on itself with panic, taking me right back to that night last winter when the fairies had held her and Father prisoner in our own palace. Spots whirled in front of my eyes. My breath thundered in my ears.

*Just let her solve this, and then I can go.*

The ice giant in the center spoke in a voice as vast and cold as an endless storm. **"You are the ruler of this kingdom?"**

His breath sent a damp chill sweeping across the square, pebbling my skin with goose bumps despite the bright sun high above us.

"No!" The king of Valmarna bustled past his guards

with his big mustache bristling in fury. He shoved Katrin aside and took her place to square off with the giant, glowering up at it. "This is *my* kingdom!" he shouted. "She's only the ruler of Drachenheim, a little nothing of a kingdom!"

The giant raised one gargantuan hand, sending showers of cold salt water raining over everyone in the square as he pointed past the king. **"And those?"** he boomed, pointing at the clustered group of royals. **"Are they rulers, too?"**

"Ah," my sister began, shifting forward. "Perhaps, King Henrik—"

"Silence!" he bellowed. "I am the one who speaks before my palace!" Puffing himself up, he set his fists on his hips. "*Those* are all the rulers of lesser kingdoms," he told the ice giants. "They've traveled from all across the continent for *my* Diamond Exhibition!"

The ice giant didn't reply. But his massive head tilted back and forth, exchanging blue-flame glances with his comrades. My stomach twisted tighter as I watched.

"Step back, Katrin," I whispered. "Step back, step back . . ."

**"All the rulers of this continent,"** said the ice giant on the left. His bluish-white lips curved within his glittering beard as his voice dropped even deeper. **"Perfect."**

"No." I didn't know what I was denying with my whisper. But my feet inched forward, carrying me closer to the nightmare against my will. "No, no—*Katrin!*"

My voice rose to a scream as the giants stretched out their hands—

And ice shot out from all their fingertips.

Katrin was the first one to be hit. A brand-new block of

ice crackled into place around her as I launched into a desperate run.

But everyone else was running now, too, and all of them were in my way. I lost sight of my sister as soldiers and mages stampeded. Sobbing and flailing, I fought forward with all my might—but everyone else was so much larger than me. Everybody else was stronger.

A sudden cry went up, piercing the chaos. I jumped up on my tiptoes, straining to see past all those taller heads . . .

And a giant block of ice rose into the sky above us, carried by two giants at once.

That block of ice was full of people.

None of them wore the black robes of battle mages or the uniforms of the Valmarene guards. No, this prison was filled with richly dressed royalty. All the visiting rulers and their families were frozen together . . . with my own sister at the far end, helplessly trapped in the ice giants' prison.

"No!" I screamed. "*Katrin!*"

The two giants who held the larger block of ice turned and marched away from the island, splashing steadily through the deep, cold seawater. Only the giant who held Jasper's mother in his grasp paused to look down at the rest of us, tiny and screaming before him.

"**No more Diamond Exhibition,**" he boomed down at us. "**No new machines for humans to invade our lands. You stay away from our realm, forever . . .**

"**Or your rulers die.**"

# CHAPTER 15

Colors and shapes whirled around me. Bodies shoved past in all directions. I couldn't take any of it in. I couldn't even look away from the too-empty sky where the giants had towered only moments ago.

I should have been in that block of ice with my sister.

I should have been in that block of ice *instead* of my sister. She wouldn't have even been here if not for me.

*"How hard could it be, for once in your life, to actually help our kingdom?"*

Because I had tossed aside all my responsibilities—because I'd wanted so badly *not* to be a princess for a few weeks of my life—my sister had been taken.

*Frozen.*

*"Katrin,"* I whispered soundlessly.

"There she is!" A male shout broke through my trance. Hard hands grabbed my arms—two pairs of hands in quick succession. Both of my guards held me now, shielding me with their bodies. "Make way for the princess!" they bellowed. "Make way for the heir to Drachenheim!"

If they hadn't held me up, I would have doubled over in agony.

I wasn't the heir to the throne. That was Katrin! That would *always* be Katrin, no matter where she was. No matter what those horrible giants might—

No. Sickness roiled through my belly. *Nothing* worse was going to happen to my sister!

No matter what happened, I knew one thing for sure: I could never be the crown princess of Drachenheim. So there was only one thing to do:

I would simply have to *get Katrin back*, for all our sakes.

"That's right," I snapped as soldiers and mages backed away from me. "I *am* a princess of Drachenheim. Now bring me whoever is in command here. Immediately!"

It was astonishing how easy it was to take charge just by snapping out orders in a confident voice, even with a tear-streaked face and student robes. Everyone else in the square must have been as flustered as I was, to comply so easily. I only had to wait a few minutes before a harried-looking woman with upswept fair hair and a peach silk gown was giving me the carefully judged curtsey of a deputy ruler to a visiting royal.

"Your Highness, I am Their Majesties' first minister, Countess Halsen. There is a great deal for me to see to at the moment, but if you would allow our guards to escort you to a safe location—"

"We're all perfectly safe," I snapped. "I'm not worried about myself. I am *concerned* about my sister!" I waved at the horizon, where the giants had disappeared into the distance. "How are you planning to get them all back?"

Countess Halsen sighed. "Your Highness, the question of what, exactly, we should do will be discussed in great detail over the next few days. In the meantime—"

"*Days?*" My own breath was suddenly choking me. "We can't wait *days*! You can't just *leave* them—"

"No?" She drew herself up to her full height. "What exactly *do* you think we should do, instead?" She was a great deal taller than I was, and her pale blue eyes were cold. "Shall we send in our armies and our best war machines to incite all our rulers' deaths immediately, when the ice giants kill them as they've promised? Is that your preference, Princess Sofia?"

"Of course not!" I muttered. "But there must be *something*. We can't just—"

"Those were *ice giants*." She shook her head as she turned away from me, not bothering with a farewell curtsey. "You may not know much about them down south, but here in the north, I can assure you: they do not make empty threats. If you genuinely care for your sister, you will pray that our council does *not* decide to mount any doomed attacks for the sake of Valmarna's honor. If we do, Princess Katrin won't survive."

She walked away without another word.

I gaped after her, heart thudding against my chest.

*Won't survive . . .*

"Your Highness?" Jurgen's voice was subdued. "Shall we?" He gestured discreetly toward the high walls of the palace.

*Of course.* Everyone expected me to wait there while the adults made their decisions. They would all keep me so wonderfully safe.

Then I'd be sent back to Drachenburg, far from danger . . . *just* like that night all those months ago when I'd been forcibly swept away to safety on a dragon's back, leaving my sister and father at the mercy of our magical invaders. That time, I hadn't been able to stop myself from being scooped away from them against my will.

*Never again.*

"Not yet." I yanked my arms firmly from both of my guards' grips. Reluctance shone from their faces as they released me; I lifted my chin higher.

What would Katrin do now?

My sister never asked anyone for their permission. Katrin simply *managed* things. Whenever she wanted something that would horrify her audience, she never said it outright; no, she approached it carefully from the side, drawing her listeners into her web of persuasion before they could realize what they'd really agreed to.

"I need to talk to Jasper before I go anywhere," I told them. "He just lost his mother, you know."

"Of course." Jurgen's broad, dark face wrinkled in

concern. "Konrad can find him for you while you and I wait in the palace—"

"No," I said. "Our alliance with the dragons is too important to risk any disrespect, especially now."

When the dragons down south discovered what had happened to Jasper's mother, their fury would be overwhelming. *They* wouldn't wait on political deliberations or be intimidated by threats. They wouldn't believe that anyone *could* ever defeat them. They'd come roaring up north with flame and claws outstretched—and there was *no* chance that they would be subtle about it.

"I have to be the one who finds Jasper first."

My guards trailed unhappily behind me as I stalked though the crowd to the far end of the square, where Jasper knelt, his fists clenched tight and his fierce golden gaze fixed on the horizon. Jurgen and Konrad shook their heads when I first waved them away, but at my glare, they reluctantly edged a foot or two farther back, giving us more space.

I only hoped it would be enough.

Jasper didn't even move as I knelt down beside him on the cold, wet tiles. The sea stretched out wide and blue before us, lapping quietly at the edges of the square. Trails of melting ice dribbled through my robe and gown.

"They took her," he said flatly, staring out at the horizon. "They just *took* her. Right in front of me! I couldn't stop them. I couldn't even get near them. I didn't even think to change shape in time." His voice dropped to a pained whisper. "Maybe Aventurine was right. I *wasn't* ready to leave the cave. What kind of dragon lets his mother be captured without a fight?"

"They took Katrin, too," I said, "and no one here is planning to get our families back—ever. They don't think there's any safe way to do it."

"So they're not even going to *try*?" Jasper's head swung around, his golden eyes burning with an inhuman flame as they latched onto mine. "They're planning to *leave them trapped in ice*? Forever?!"

It must have been the worst fate imaginable for a fire-breathing dragon.

"It might be worse," I told him. "If they decide to go after them with war machines blazing, just to prove a point—"

"Then the giants will kill our families." Jasper's teeth gnashed together. "They'll never miss a whole army coming to attack!"

"*Or* a pack of dragons," I told him, dropping my voice to a whisper. "But—if we hurry—I think I can find a way for us to travel there, ourselves, in secret."

"Oh?" Jasper's eyes narrowed. He leaned close. "How?"

My guards shifted nearer. I scowled and shooed them back.

Then I whispered the words directly into Jasper's ear. "How much space do you need to change shapes?"

His eyes flashed with deep golden sparks. "I can change in midair if no one's in my way."

I almost laughed as I gestured at the deep water just in front of us. "I don't see anyone blocking us. Do you?"

His lips curved into a dangerous smile. "My scales

haven't hardened yet," he warned me. "If any of those battle mages or soldiers attack—"

"If they do, it'll be a declaration of war on Drachenheim." I worried at my lower lip as I glanced across the square full of milling, frightened people. Would they remember those political implications right now? Or would they panic and forget?

My gaze fell on my sister's carriage, still waiting nearby. "I know exactly how to remind them."

I rose to my feet, shaking out my sodden skirts, and nodded to my younger guard. "Could you bring me our flag, please, Konrad?"

Looking relieved, he gave a martial nod and marched briskly across the square.

Jurgen's frown only deepened, though. As Konrad returned and passed me the big, brightly colored cloth, Jurgen said, "Your Highness, may I ask—?"

"Step back," I ordered both of them. "I need to make an announcement on behalf of our kingdom."

Wincing, Jurgen eased slowly backward. Konrad followed, looking confused. Ulrike bustled up behind them, her eyes wide. "Your Highness, take care! You're standing *so* close to the water. It can't be safe! Why don't you come inside the palace, where I can find you a hot drink and—"

"Shh," I told her gently. "Jasper?"

He was standing beside me now. "I'm ready."

Jaw clenched, he turned his back on me. Still clutching the flag against my chest, I grabbed his closest shoulder, yanked myself up onto his narrow back—

And he leaped high into the air, shifting forms.

Screams and shouts ripped across the square.

I flung out the flag of Drachenheim as Jasper's wide, scaly body settled into place beneath me. His great purple-and-blue wings beat strongly around us, sending gusts of wind billowing against my long blue robe and stretching my nation's flag high in the air for all to see.

My guards' faces turned into masks of horror far below. "*Don't you dare follow us,*" I shouted down at the top of my lungs. "*That's a royal order! And while we're gone . . .*"

I struggled for the right words, the clever, careful words that I needed to direct them all in just the right way. But all the diplomatic skills in our family belonged to my sister, and I was the only princess of Drachenheim left. So:

"*Don't do anything stupid!*" I bellowed down to the square full of mages and soldiers and high ministers.

Jasper tucked his legs beneath his body and shot forward over the wide, glittering blue water . . .

And for the second time in my life, I soared away from chaos on dragonback. This time, though, I wasn't being swept away from danger.

I was heading straight toward it.

# CHAPTER 16

"Which way?" Jasper's voice sounded deeper and harsher in dragon form, filled with the rumbling echoes of a growl. As he tilted his long neck to peer back at me, though, his bright golden eyes shone, warm and familiar, in the midst of his ferocious, scaly face.

Terror was a cold clamp around my spine, but for once, it had nothing to do with flying on a dragon. I'd read every one of Jasper's letters again and again. I *knew* he wouldn't let me fall.

"We have to find my friends," I told him, locking my legs firmly into place around his back. "They were on their way out of the city. Do you think you can pick them out from the air? Or would that be too difficult?"

"Pfft." Twin balls of smoke shot out of Jasper's long

snout as he snorted. "I could spy a mouse from two miles away! I can certainly hunt down a whole pack of goblins."

And it took less than ten minutes of circling the islands of Villenne before he snarled, "Got them!"

Tucking his wings around my legs, he veered downward in a tightly aimed dive toward one of the farthest islands . . . where a group of tiny dots revealed themselves to be a group of green goblins hurrying along a wide, barely paved road toward the final bridge to the mainland.

"Talvikki! Berrit! Hannalena! Fedolia!" I shouted as we shot toward the ground, goblins shrieking and scattering out of our way. "It's me! Sofia! I'm—"

"*Sofi?*" Berrit popped into view below, staring up in amazement. "What in the world—?"

"Well, that explains why he didn't smell like a human!" Talvikki appeared on the street beside her, shaking her head as we landed with a thud that sent abandoned shop carts flying in every direction. "Sofi," she said, "you are full of surprises."

Berrit edged backward, her eyes fixed on Jasper's open mouth. "He's not going to eat us, is he?"

"Of course not!" I gave Jasper a reassuring pat as he huffed in disgust. "He's a philosopher. Just like us."

"'Us'?" Hannalena repeated as she and Fedolia finally appeared behind the others. Her thoughtful gaze fixed on the flag that pooled on the ground beside me, where I'd dropped it as we'd landed. "I think our Sofi may have been keeping secrets from us, girls."

Something dangerous glittered in Fedolia's blue eyes.

"Ooh, now, that *is* interesting. And here we all thought we'd finally found a human who might actually be trustworthy!"

A low growl rumbled up Jasper's long throat. Berrit stepped away hastily, her eyes widening.

"It's all right," I told them both. "Just let me explain."

Luckily, every one of my friends loved gossip. All the goblin girls gathered close around me as I lowered my voice, while Fedolia listened from one pointed step away. The other goblins disappeared into the distance, and the local humans peered suspiciously at us all through their closed windows.

Street guards would have come to investigate us in any of Villenne's wealthier islands—but here, with ancient paint peeling off the tall, rickety houses and every human hiding inside them, we were left to ourselves as I told the whole story.

"So you're a princess," Berrit said at last, putting the pieces together as meticulously as always. "A future queen. That's . . . not what I'd expected."

Talvikki let out a crack of laughter and leaned her head affectionately against my shoulder. Despite all my fears over the last few days, she had forgiven my deception immediately. I *knew* I should have told her days ago. "She'll be the first human queen to have shared cinnamon rolls with any goblins, that's for sure!"

"I will *never* be the queen of Drachenheim," I said firmly. "We're going to get my sister back."

Fedolia's eyes narrowed into blue slits. Even Hannalena looked pained. "Sofi, if you knew more about ice giants—"

"*You* do, don't you?" I looked around their familiar faces, my whole body tight with desperation. "You've dealt with them before. That's why we came to you for help!"

"But we *ran* from them," Talvikki said. "Why do you think we didn't leave Villenne by the tunnels? Every goblin tunnel ever built up north was smashed into pieces. *That's* what they do whenever we try to get anywhere near them."

"But—"

"Do you have any idea what a cave-in is like?" Hannalena demanded. "Or the other kinds of destruction they can wreak? We *warned* you to run. If you'd taken our advice—"

"But they're gone now!" said Berrit brightly. "And because of Sofi, we know they won't be coming back, either. They only stomped over here for those humans! So we'll be perfectly safe going back to Scholars' Island and—"

"My *mother* isn't safe!" Jasper snarled, his long tail lashing against the street. "Neither is Sofia's sister! Or any of the others! Sofia was the only royal who escaped."

"Well . . . royals . . ." Hannalena's wide shoulders shifted in a shrug. "They're always used as hostages or symbols, aren't they? Being trapped in ice at least means they won't be *hurt*, so—"

"I *am not leaving my mother frozen in ice!*" Windows shivered and broke all down the street at Jasper's roar. Humans screamed inside the shaking wooden houses. He reared up, wings mantling, and bellowed down at all of us: "Dragons *protect* their families!"

"So do goblins," Hannalena said flatly, glowering back

at him. "That's why we swore never to go near any ice giants again. You need to understand: they *cannot be defeated.* They don't even keep their hearts in their own bodies! They keep them safely hidden, so *nothing* you do can ever hurt them. It is pointless to even try to fight!"

Hands fisted by her sides, she turned back to me. "I am sorry for your loss, Sofi. I expect you'll need to go back to your own kingdom, but if you want to stay with us a while first—"

"I'm not going without my sister," I told her. "My kingdom doesn't need me. It needs her."

Talvikki frowned. "What's wrong with you?"

If she'd ever met me in my true habitat, she wouldn't need to ask. "Never mind that," I said. "We need to head north before the Valmarene army can do anything catastrophically stupid. If you really won't come with us, will you at least give us directions?"

"They can sense every rumble of stone underground," Berrit said with soft intensity. "That's how they found all our tunnels—and they left *none* intact. They cared nothing for our families' screams. And they'll see you if you fly through the air. There is *no way* to sneak around them."

"We-e-ell . . ." Fedolia flicked a speck of dust off her robe with one long, pointed blue fingernail. "There might be *one* way . . . but only if you were willing to enter into a little bargain with me."

She lowered one ghost-white eyelid in a wink as she met my gaze for the first time I could remember. "No one ever sees *me* if I don't want them to. I can lead you to the ice giants *and* keep you invisible along the way. And since you *aren't* an ordinary human as you'd claimed . . ."

Her blue lips twisted bitterly. "I do quite like the idea of a real human queen owing *me* a favor as my half of the deal. So . . ." She cocked her head and stroked her fingers across the silver chain that hung around her neck. "What do you say, *Princess Sofia of Drachenheim*? Will you agree to that bargain?"

I took a deep breath as I looked down into her enigmatic blue eyes.

Fedolia didn't like me. I couldn't even guess what she was really thinking right now.

But she *had* rescued two of the ice giants' prisoners already. She'd risked everything to help Talvikki's cousins escape—and she'd lost everything for it, too. That had to prove something.

All the goblin girls were frowning now, though, as they looked between us. Talvikki shook her head at me, her green face scrunched up in concern, and I knew exactly what was bothering her.

One thing was true for every magical creature: their bargains, once set, were *unbreakable*. If I agreed to this now and Fedolia kept her side of the bargain, I would *have* to grant whatever favor she asked me afterward, no matter how awful it might be . . . and with Fedolia, I couldn't even begin to guess.

"*She's fond of tricks and pranks.*" That's what Talvikki had told me, wasn't it?

But if I didn't agree, I'd end up responsible for *all* of Drachenheim's risky decisions in the future.

"I will never be queen," I told her firmly, "but Drachenheim *will* owe you a favor, I promise. Jasper can tell you: we don't break our alliances."

"*Excellent*," Fedolia purred. "Then if your dragon can handle all the flying, I'll keep us from being seen on the way there." She let out a high, tinkling laugh as she sauntered past me and gave Jasper's scaly side a condescending pat. "This should be even more fun than a riot!"

My stomach churned as I followed after her ... and I hoped I hadn't just made another mistake that my whole kingdom would regret.

# CHAPTER 17

I hadn't thought about the cold.

When we first took off, soaring high above Villenne, my gown and student robe were still sodden with salt water, but the summer sun shone down on us, and Jasper's scales radiated heat. As the sky darkened around us, though, a growing chill crept through my sticky-stiff clothes, growing more and more intense with every minute. Each new beat of Jasper's wings sent an icy blast through me. I hunched lower and lower over his warm back. It wasn't enough. By the time the sky turned fully black, I was shivering uncontrollably.

"Better get used to it, Princess." Fedolia was perched on the curve of Jasper's shoulder in front of me. I could just make out the shift of her shadowy silhouette as she swung her legs casually in midair. "It'll get a lot colder soon enough!"

"Are you cold, Sofia?" Jasper's head swung around, his long neck twisting like a snake. His eyes glowed gold in the darkness, like eerie lamps. "I could blow smoke on you if it would help."

"No, thank you." I grimaced, wrapping my arms around my chest. My stomach was growling; it hadn't occurred to me to bring food, either. I clenched my teeth to stop their telltale chattering.

"We should land soon anyway," Jasper said. "I've never flown so far in just one day. My wings . . . they're still not fully developed." A gust of smoke escaped his mouth as he let out a hissing sigh. "If I go much farther, they'll be too sore to even lift us off the ground tomorrow."

*What?* As miserable as I was, my head still snapped up in horror. We couldn't just stop! Not when our families were locked in ice!

But the last time I'd let my temper loose, I'd lost *everything* . . . so I forced back my instinctive, furious protest and kept my mouth clamped tightly shut as Jasper arced down through the vast, cold darkness toward the grassy top of a massive, treeless hill. He landed with a crash that jolted through my aching bones, and his wings sagged limply to the ground.

"Hmm!" Fedolia hopped off easily from his shoulders, dusting her hands together and letting off blue sparks. "You certainly could do with a bit more practice, dragon-boy."

Jasper let out a weary growl, his big head sinking down to lie flat on the ground. The golden lamplight of his gaze snapped off as his eyes fell closed.

*Thank goodness.* I did not want him to see this.

Slowly, painfully, I slid down the broad curve of his back, my robe and skirts snagging again and again on his scales. Finally, I landed on two feet again—and staggered hard, pain lancing through my body.

Every single piece of me *hurt*! I'd spent so many hours braced around his big dragon back that the muscles in my legs, my back, my neck—and even my face!—all seemed to scream out in agony as I tried to un-clench.

I couldn't even force my legs to straighten.

And—*gaah*. Of course I hadn't brought a chamber pot, either.

Shuffling like an old woman and biting back a moan, I turned to scan the countryside around us. Clouds had shifted away from the moon as we'd landed. By its faint glow, I could see a lake spread out on one side of the hill, reflecting the bright stars in its dark waters. Far in the distance, on the other side of the hill, I could just make out a small patch of scattered lights—a village, perhaps? I couldn't have walked that far even if I weren't an aching lump of knotted muscles.

Fedolia had been right: it was already *much* colder here than it had been in Villenne. And there was nothing to protect us from the biting wind on this high, bare hilltop.

I'd spent so much time resenting my ladies-in-waiting for the way they'd been forced on me. But I'd never actually thought about the way they looked after me ... until now. *Ulrike* would have thought to pack warm clothes and something to eat for the journey. I'd never packed for myself in my life.

"I'm off!" Fedolia announced—and vanished.

*What?*

I stared, mind reeling, at the empty patch of grass where she had stood.

"Do you think she's coming back?" Jasper rumbled. He'd only half opened his eyes at her announcement. Even his voice was drooping, his words sliding into hisses on his long, forked tongue.

"Who knows?" I shrugged helplessly as cold wind whistled through my gritty, sticky gown. "I don't even know if she's really gone."

Maybe she'd only wanted some privacy. Then again, perhaps she'd changed her mind about the whole adventure and started back toward Villenne on her own. I didn't understand anything about that kobold.

Another gust of cold wind billowed across the hilltop. This time, I stumbled with the force of it.

*Enough.* I was so worn out, I could barely even think. But I knew one thing: I wouldn't do my sister any good by letting myself freeze on this hillside.

Grimacing, I stumped over to Jasper's big, bulky body. "Would you mind—?"

"Of course." He heaved up his closest wing to make space.

"*Ohhh.*" I collapsed onto the grass beside him with a groan, tucking myself tightly against his hot scales. His wing drifted back down to cover me like a hot, scratchy blanket, and I closed my eyes, letting my head sink against his side. It moved gently up and down with his breath, rocking me backward and forward.

Three weeks ago, being so close to anyone would have made me stiffen with panicky discomfort. Now, as I let myself be rocked like an infant, my breathing gradually eased. My shoulders ached even more as they finally began to loosen.

Hunger gnawed at my empty stomach. I would have spent my whole quarterly allowance to buy a single cinnamon roll right now. I would have given my entire library for a chamber pot!

But for the first time since I'd seen my sister's carriage flying toward us that morning, I felt almost...safe. So I couldn't hold back the words any longer. "I'm sorry."

It was the first time I'd willingly apologized in my life. The words slipped out in a shamed whisper.

Had he even heard me? He didn't say anything. I held my breath as I waited through the long, agonizing silence.

Finally, he shifted behind me. "Sorry for what?"

"Do you have to ask?" When I reopened my eyes, I found his big head tilted over me and his golden gaze focused intently on me. "If I'd stayed with the others in the palace, the way I was supposed to, you'd be safe underneath your mountain right now. Your mother would be safe there, too."

"But not for long." His tone was thoughtful. "If you were the one who'd been taken today instead of your sister, my mother would have flown after the giants to retrieve you. Our honor—and our alliance—would have required it."

"Well..." I heaved a sigh. "Maybe she wouldn't have been captured, though. Or—"

"You think she would have attacked them any differently?" His head tilted even more, the pupils of his eyes narrowing into vertical, reptilian slits. "I told you how my family defines power: *flame and claws.* She would never have brought any other weapons to a battle."

"But—oh, this is absurd!" I flapped one hand in frustration beneath his heavy wing. "How can you *not* blame me for everything that's gone wrong? I'm the whole reason you're here!"

His shrug rolled all the way down his huge body. "Did you trick me into sneaking out of my cavern to meet you? Did you even *ask* me to do it in the first place?"

I scowled, digging myself deeper into the warmth of his scaly side. "Didn't I say in my letter that I wished you were with me?"

His laugh sent balls of smoke flying from his snout. "You think I took that as an *order*?" Jasper tipped back his head, showing off all his teeth in his grin. "You do remember I'm a dragon, don't you?"

"Hmmph." I crossed my arms and stuck my jaw out. "I'm just *trying* to apologize for getting you into trouble!"

"Oh, really." Jasper snorted. "You think too much like a princess."

"*What?*" In all the *many* criticisms I'd had leveled against me in my life, no one had ever once claimed that.

"You think everything is your responsibility."

"Just ask my sister," I muttered. "She'll tell you I don't *have* any sense of responsibility."

"Then she hasn't been paying attention." Jasper curved his neck fully around to look at me face-to-face, his hot breath steaming the last chills from my skin. "You told me how Gert van Heidecker defined power. Remember? He said it only exists when wielded over other people. Well, *you* couldn't control my decision to come here, *or* what the ice giants did, could you? So you don't have that much power... *or* that much responsibility. You see?"

He gave another rolling shrug that bounced my head against his side as he settled his chin back down on his front feet with a sigh. "It's all because of the princess problem."

"*The princess problem?*" I groaned. "If you're trying to tell me I'm no good at being a princess—"

"No, you're too good a princess," he said calmly. "When you get upset, you forget to think like a philosopher. It's not your fault, though. You've been told all your life that you're more important than anyone else only because of the family you were born into. I *told* you humans are all obsessed with blood."

"We are not—!" I took a deep breath. *No more losing my temper!* "I'm not more important *as a person*," I gritted. "But as a princess, I *do* have more responsibilities than other people, because my whole kingdom can suffer for my actions." My shoulders hunched as I repeated the reminder that had battered me endlessly across the years.

"But why is *this* your fault?" Jasper said. "What could *you* possibly have done to stop the ice giants today?"

"What about you?" I twisted around, glowering at him. "*You* said your mother would have been captured no matter when she went after the ice giants. But look at you now! You're going after them, too. Do you think *you* have any more power than she does?"

"That's different." His voice dropped to a dangerous pitch.

"How?" I demanded.

"She's my *mother*." His deep, ominous growl probably should have frightened me. But we'd been arguing philosophy by post for months, and besides: I'd already been inside one dragon's mouth. Being shouted at by another couldn't frighten me. "I'm not leaving her trapped in ice!" he roared.

Strands of my hair flew out of their pins with the gust of his hot breath.

"Because you have a *responsibility* to her," I said triumphantly, shaking my finger at him. "You see? Just like I have a responsibility to my kingdom!"

"Ha!" He snorted out a smoke ring that bounced off my face. "So this has *nothing* to do with saving your sister just because you love your family?"

"My *family*—!" I cut myself off, breathing hard. Katrin's last words to me rang in my ears.

"I *will never, ever forgive you for this*."

I'd always known we weren't like other families I'd met, even before today's disaster. But now . . .

I curled my fingers into fists, shoving those thoughts deep down where they couldn't hurt me. "I'm saving my sister *for our kingdom*," I snarled, "because Drachenheim needs her in charge—and ensuring my kingdom's future is *my* responsibility. So maybe princesses *aren't* such a problem!"

"My goodness!" a third voice chirped, making me jump. "It looks like I've missed the best entertainment this evening!"

Fedolia popped back into sight beside us, her expression

glittering with interest in the lamplight of Jasper's eyes. "I was just eating my supper. *Delicious* fish in the lake down below! They're nice and lively, I can tell you. They really wriggle as they slide down your throat!" She cocked her head to one side. "Aren't you two going to go fish for your own suppers? Or would you prefer to argue a while longer? I never mind some good theater before bed!"

Sitting down cross-legged on the cold grass, she looked at us both expectantly.

Apparently, tonight *could* get worse after all ... but I'd finally been pushed too far to care. Nudging Jasper's wing firmly aside, I rose to my feet. "I am going for a walk," I announced. "*Do not* look where I'm going. I mean it!"

Jasper's wings lifted off the ground. "Don't you think you should have company? For safety—"

"No." I glared menacingly at him. "I want to be alone. So *no looking,* either of you!"

I might be used to being on display for the good of my kingdom. But some things were private even for a princess.

I couldn't save my sister tonight, convince Jasper of the most basic truths in my world, or catch live fish to eat with my hands ...

But I was determined to figure out life without a chamber pot, because I desperately needed to feel relief about *something,* and that was the only option I had left.

# CHAPTER 18

That night, I didn't even try to sleep. As Jasper's snores rumbled across the hilltop and Fedolia slept curled up on top of him, I crunched myself into a ball against his hot, scaly side. My arms wrapped tightly around my legs, but they weren't nearly enough to ward off danger.

Scenes from the day flashed over and over again behind my eyelids in an unstoppable, nightmarish progression. I had to clamp my lips shut to keep myself from screaming out loud to make them *stop*.

Katrin's face as she had shouted at me . . .

The ice giants carrying her away . . .

Moaning, I buried my head against my knees. If only I was an ice giant. Keeping my heart safely hidden where no one else could touch it would make everything in my life *so* much easier.

It would have helped if my cat from Villenne were here, curled in the spot that he'd claimed every night since we'd arrived. Feeling his low, soothing purr vibrate against my chest always made me feel calmer about *everything*. I could have thought so much more clearly with his fluffy weight nestled beside me.

I'd probably never see him again.

I should have taken the time to name him while I'd had him. Somehow, though, I'd persuaded myself it wouldn't hurt so much to lose him when we left Villenne if I'd never given him a name in the first place.

I should have done so many things differently. All I could do now, though, was decide what to do next . . . and by the time the others woke up in the morning, I was ready.

"Right!" As Jasper slowly blinked his eyes open and Fedolia stretched luxuriantly, still perched on his back, I pushed my aching body to my feet and smacked my hands together. There was a hot, grainy feeling behind my eyes, the back of my mouth tasted sour, and the world spun unnervingly every time I moved, sending a nasty sloshing feeling through my empty stomach. But I kept my expression firm, like a real ruler. "First, we need breakfast," I announced. "All of us."

Jasper opened his mouth in a yawn that exposed far too much of his long tongue and let out a bad stench of his own. "You want to go hunting?" he asked sleepily. "It might take me a few hours, but—"

"Fedolia can fish for all of us," I said. "She's the fastest and the best at it."

"Why, thank you." Fedolia's upper lip curled into a sneer. "And yet—"

"Jasper, you'll do the cooking." There was *no way* I was going to eat a live fish—or even a raw one. Getting sick was the last thing I needed right now! Fortunately, partway through the night, I had finally realized that I had a ready source of cooking fire snoring just beside me.

"Me?" Jasper looked suddenly alert—and alarmed. "My sister's the one who knows how to cook food. I've never—"

"Think of it as practice for spending time as a human," I told him. "We *always* cook our meat. It's a rule."

Fedolia's long blue fingernails tapped—*click! click! click!*—against Jasper's blue-and-purple scales as she glared down at me. "And you, Your Highness?" she asked with poisonous sweetness. "How exactly are *you* planning to contribute this morning, while we run about following your royal orders?"

I took a deep breath and stiffened my back. *No more cowardice.* "I'm going to become a criminal," I announced. "But I'll need help from both of you to do it."

Fedolia's blue eyes widened. She blinked. Then her light blue lips stretched into a grin of malicious delight. "*Finally,*" she said, "a plan I can really enjoy!"

Less than two hours later, Jasper circled through the air while I squeezed my legs around his back for balance and clung to Fedolia's shoulders with both hands. All three of us were hidden by her invisibility spell . . . but my heart raced faster and faster with every moment we came closer to implementing my plan.

Only a month ago, I'd planned to spend the rest of my life safely locked inside the walls of my palace. How had everything gone so wildly off course?

"There!" Fedolia leaned over Jasper's side, tugging me with her, to point down at a scattered group of cottages around an empty green square. Farmland stretched out in a wide circle around them, and I glimpsed men and women alike out working in the fields. "It's washing day," Fedolia said. "Perfect!"

*Unbelievable.* Woolens and furs flapped freely in the breeze, suspended from plain ropes behind the houses without a single guard set to protect them.

Wasn't anyone worried about thieves like me?

"That grassy space is big enough for me to land," Jasper said thoughtfully. "But if anyone sees me, you know they'll panic."

"That's all right." Fedolia settled back into place, nestling her back against my front and propping her crossed ankles on Jasper's neck. "I'll stay with you, dragon-boy. We'll keep you safely hidden while Sofi goes on her crime spree."

"*What?*" I spat out a mouthful of her wind-tossed white hair from between my lips, my heart giving a sickly lurch. My entire plan had been based on being invisible!

"Humans do get silly about dragons," Fedolia said regretfully. "Of course *we* know he won't eat any of them, because he's a philosopher and a gentleman. But unless you *want* them shooting a whole storm of arrows before he can explain anything—"

"No." I tightened my legs around Jasper's scales. They wouldn't be hardened for decades yet. A plain human arrow could go right through them! "This is *my* plan," I said. "I'll take the risk. But . . ." I swallowed hard.

*This is for Drachenheim. Remember?* Still, my voice came out sounding pathetically small. "Don't leave without me, will you? No matter what happens while we're there?"

"Sofia." Jasper's neck curved until he was looking back at me with one glinting, golden eye. "I *told* you: dragons always protect their territory!"

"I beg your pardon?" A half laugh burst out from my tight chest, despite my panic. "You think your *friends* count as your territory?" Snorting, I shook my head at him, feeling my heart rate finally re-settle as philosophy saved me yet again. "Obviously, we have a *lot* to discuss as soon as this is finished!"

But first, I had to embark on my brand-new life of crime.

As Jasper thumped down onto the village square, I slid off his back before I could think twice about it. Then I stopped, blinking rapidly. He had completely disappeared from my vision. It looked as if my hands were flattened against empty air.

Suddenly, every window on every tiny stone cottage around the grassy square felt like a wide-open eye staring directly at me.

"Sorry," Fedolia's voice caroled through the empty air.

"You aren't touching me anymore, so you aren't covered by my spell."

I frowned, my memory twanging with dissonance. "I'm touching Jasper, though. And that first day in Villenne, when we met, didn't you cast it over all of us without needing to—"

"D'you think you know more about kobold magic than I do?" Fedolia's cool fingers tapped impatiently against mine. For just a moment, I glimpsed her lying flat on her stomach on Jasper's back, waving her other hand at me in a shoo-ing gesture. "Just go!" she told me as she blinked back out of view. "And for goodness' sake, stop looking so suspicious!"

"How can I *not* look suspicious?" I hissed at the space where she had been. "I just appeared in the middle of their village, out of nowhere!"

"If you stand around dithering, they'll *all* catch sight of you on their way home for lunch."

*Argh!* My breath panted in and out in short spurts as I unpeeled my fingers from the security of Jasper's invisible scales.

"Go on." His voice rumbled encouragingly through the air. "If I could pass as an ordinary human in Villenne, you can certainly do it now!"

There had been *nothing* ordinary about the way that Jasper had looked or acted in human form. But a curtain twitched in the corner of my vision, and it spurred me into motion before I could explain *exactly* how wrong he was about everything.

*Later*, I promised myself, and stalked across the grass

toward the closest cottage, doing my best not to look suspicious.

*Of course* I belonged here in this tiny village in the middle of nowhere, where no one had ever seen me before. *Of course* there was nothing to suspect as I crossed their quiet square in a bright blue university robe. I looked perfectly calm and casual and—

A door clicked open, and I took off like a startled mouse, yanking up my skirts and robe and racing between the closest two cottages to flatten myself against a cold side wall.

"Hello?" a woman's voice called out. "Is anybody there?"

There was a long pause. My heartbeat rattled against my chest. I pressed my lips frantically together.

"Huh. Must've imagined it."

The door closed. I slumped with relief, putting one hand to my chest as I struggled to catch my breath. I was *so* not suited to a criminal life!

*Dear Katrin.* Closing my eyes, I began to compose a new letter in my mind. *You'll be glad to know I'm a failure at crime as well as politics and courtly etiquette . . .*

A door slammed open just inside the cottage I was leaning against. I spun around.

I couldn't see anyone. But a moment later, a cheerful, tuneless whistle sounded through the closest window. As I waited, paralyzed with horror, it came closer and closer . . . and then moved away again. The door inside the cottage opened and shut.

How did professional thieves survive this kind of

terror? I drew a deep breath, my whole body trembling, and then dashed out to the grass behind the cottage before panic could stop my non-criminal heart entirely.

There was no time to be fussy. I lunged at the first woollen shawl I saw on the clothesline and yanked hard.

It didn't move. Something was holding it—

*Aha.* I fumbled with the odd-looking wooden clamp that trapped it against the line. *There!* I slung the shawl triumphantly across my shoulder. Next to its spot on the line hung a set of big, male undergarments—*ugh!*—and then a pair of long, striped knitted tights, which I quickly added to my collection. Then a thick red woollen petticoat, a long scarf, an oversized woollen shirt, and—

"Oy!" A window slammed open behind me, and a woman's voice bellowed, "You! Stop right there! What are you doing with my laundry?"

I bolted before she even finished her question, tripping and stumbling over my skirts and my long student robe while I clutched my stack of ill-gotten goods in my arms.

The front door crashed open as I rounded the corner of the cottage, still a good ten feet from the village green. *Don't pause to look!*

But I couldn't help myself.

The woman glowering out at me from the doorway was huge! I'd never seen such muscular arms, not even on my guards. If only Jurgen and Konrad were here now! They might be treacherous, sneaking tattletales, but I would have given anything to have them with me at that moment.

There was no one to protect me as I lurched desperately

toward the village green, crying out with frustration as my feet caught on the hem of my skirt *yet again* and that red-faced, strong-armed woman marched toward me, rolling up her sleeves in preparation.

Hot breath scorched my skin at the edge of the grass. "Quickly! Up on my back!"

Jasper might have been whispering by dragon standards, but the force of his hiss blew back my hair and sent my pursuer lurching backward in shock. "What in the world—?" She stopped and stared wildly around the empty-looking square, obviously searching for the source of that massive whisper.

I lunged forward until I hit Jasper's invisible side, and then I shoved my pile of clothing as high as I could.

"Got 'em!" invisible Fedolia called cheerfully as she yanked them from my grasp.

"What is going on?" the woman behind me demanded as my stolen pile disappeared from view. "Who *are* you, anyway?"

"I'm sorry!" I said miserably, scrabbling for a foothold. It was *hard* to climb when I couldn't see the scales in front of me! Jasper gave a muted roar of pain as I accidentally stepped on his wing. I cringed. "Sorry, sorry!" I repeated to both of them. "I *am* really sorry. For everything!"

Until last night, I had never willingly apologized in my life. But right now my usual resistance fell away, as front doors opened all around the square and villagers flooded out to watch me climb into apparently empty air.

"But my clothes!" At least the woman wasn't chasing me

anymore. She just gaped at me, shaking her head in disbelief. "How—what—?"

*There!* I finally found a good toehold on Jasper's side. I scrambled up as quickly as I could—and a cool hand fastened around my arm. Fedolia! I let out a sob of sheer relief. *Finally.*

Jasper and Fedolia both snapped into view—and the woman let out a shout of rage as I disappeared.

"Thief!" she shouted. "Sneaky, magical thief!" She charged forward, her face purpling.

Jasper bunched his legs beneath him in preparation to launch. I yanked my purse from my skirts in desperation as I climbed into place behind Fedolia.

"Here!" I shouted, tossing it back toward the woman just before she could reach us. "Take this! You can have it! And I really am sorr—*eeee!*"

My voice cracked into a scream as Jasper leaped into the air.

I slid helplessly down his back, losing my grip entirely.

Villagers shouted from below as I snapped back into view. I threw myself forward, wrapping my arms and legs around Jasper's back . . .

. . . And Fedolia shrieked with laughter as we sailed high above the village green, leaving the scene of my crime behind forever.

Ripples of aftershock flooded my body. My teeth chattered wildly as I pressed my face against Jasper's hot scales. "I can't believe I did that. I can't believe I—"

"Wooo!" Fedolia twirled my stolen shawl triumphantly.

"Talvikki was right—you *do* have guts after all! I can't believe it either!" Her chain had slipped free from her student robe in our take-off, and a massive blue pendant—a fist-sized chunk of blue topaz?—bounced against her chest as if it were dancing, too, as the world tilted dizzyingly below us.

"Auggggh," I moaned, and squeezed my eyes shut against the view.

"What was that thing you tossed down at the end?" Jasper called back. His wings beat strongly around us as his body leveled out. "A rock? Or—"

"Just my purse." Groaning, I pulled my weary, aching body into a sitting position, taking deep, slow breaths of cold air to settle my stomach. "There wasn't much inside it, though," I added regretfully.

My guards were the ones who always handled my payments, but I'd glanced inside it this morning just in case. So, for once, I had some idea of the amount. "There were only seven or eight gold pieces in there," I admitted. "That's why I knew there'd be no point in trying to *buy* enough clothing to keep me warm."

"Seven or eight gold pieces?" Fedolia repeated incredulously. "Sofi!" Tipping back her head, she gave a wild cackle of pure delight. "You are *the worst* thief ever. No one in their right mind would pay a *single* gold piece for this entire pile!"

"What?" I stared at her, my mouth dropping open. "But—"

"Thirteen krügen," she said. "That's what I'd pay for all of these. At *most!*" Still chortling, she held up my precious, stolen clothes like a pile of dirty rags on their way to the fire. "All the same . . ."

Her smile turned rueful as I snatched them away from her and cuddled them protectively to my chest. "We might just make it all the way up north after all," she finished, tucking her big blue pendant back under her robes, "now that you're not so likely to freeze along the way."

"We'd *better* make it all the way up there." I wrapped the shawl tightly around my shoulders as even more tremors rippled through me.

I *hated* looking stupid ... and I'd just been proven an idiot at practical matters once again.

The moment I got Katrin safely home, I was going to climb inside my bedcovers with a delicious pot of hot chocolate and a pile of books and never leave my room again ... because clearly, I couldn't manage life in the outside world at all.

# CHAPTER 19

My stolen clothes were worth every coin I'd paid for them. As Jasper's wings swept us farther and farther north, the air filled with gusts of whirling snow. Sheets of ice spread across the landscape below, and I huddled inside all my layers at once, like an animal growing thick winter fur.

I would have shared my hoard with Fedolia, but she laughed derisively when I made the reluctant offer.

"I'm a beautiful *kobold*, not a human! D'you think I need all that nonsense to stay warm?"

She certainly didn't seem bothered as she jumped up on tiptoes on Jasper's back and gathered up wet, cold handfuls of the swirling snow that fell around us as we flew. Patting it around her cheeks and face, she laughed and wriggled with delight. I looked away, shivering, and clung closer to Jasper's hot scales, where the snow melted with a hiss on impact.

I would never understand that kobold.

And I was taken entirely off guard a moment later when she dropped suddenly down and grabbed hold of my leg with a wet, cold hand, snapping invisibility around all of us without warning.

"Wha—?" I began, my voice muffled by my scarf.

Her other hand slammed over my mouth, sharp blue fingernails digging through the wool into my cheek. Snow melted through to nip my skin with cold as I stared at her.

I couldn't hear anything but the slow *swish-swish* of Jasper's wings beating steadily through the air and the soft hiss of snow falling around us. But Fedolia's long, pointed white ears swiveled sideways as I watched, following some sound I couldn't catch. Lifting her hand from my leg, she worried frantically at the silver chain around her neck, fingers rubbing back and forth against it as if it were a good-luck charm.

With her hand gripping my face, I couldn't even crane over Jasper's side to see what was happening below. There could be ice giants moving around *just beneath us*, waiting to freeze us the moment they saw through her spell! Or—

"Phew." Fedolia sagged against me, letting go of my cheeks and giving her necklace a final, reassuring pat. "That was close."

"*What* was close?" Yanking off my scarf, I breathed in as deeply as I could. "What just *happened*?"

Fedolia's face tightened. "You don't need to know."

"*I'd* like to know anyway," Jasper rumbled ahead of us.

"You are *not* keeping this a secret." I crossed my arms over my chest and narrowed my eyes at the kobold, who was plucking a strand of red scarf-wool from one of her long blue nails with intense concentration. "Out with it!"

She sighed heavily, without looking up. "It has nothing to do with ice giants *or* your families."

"So?"

"Fine!" A streak of shocking bright blue appeared on her cheeks for the first time ever. Was the fearless, sharp-tongued kobold girl actually *blushing*? "It was *my* family," she muttered. "You see? Not your problem!"

"*Your* family?" I wriggled so quickly to the side that I nearly slid off—but I had practice, by now, at riding on dragonback. So I kept my seat as I peered behind Jasper's wings to the ground below.

It was empty. Only white snow and ice stretched as far as I could see.

"You won't see them *now*," Fedolia said impatiently. "We only passed them on their way back down to the mine."

"The *mine*?" I repeated blankly. "I thought the kobolds up here were all spies for the ice giants."

"You—!" Her mouth dropped open, shock mingling with outrage on her face. "What do *you* know about kobolds? Or any of this?"

*Uh-oh.* Fedolia did like her secrets . . . so she probably *wouldn't* be happy at all to know that Talvikki and I had talked about her. I shrugged, trying my best to look casual. "I just . . . heard that that's why the giants let the kobolds stay, to help protect their hidden hearts. And *that's* why you couldn't stay anymore—because you were kinder-hearted than the rest of your family."

"There is *nothing wrong* with my family!" She glared murderously at me.

"Then why are we avoiding them?" Jasper inquired. "Do you want to go down and find them now?" He started to curve around in midair.

"No!" She grabbed hold of the chain around her neck and twisted it in her hands. "I *can't.* You don't understand, either of you!"

I scowled, crossing my arms. I hated not understanding things! "Explain it, then. Weren't you thrown out because you were kind enough to help the goblins?"

"I was thrown out," she snapped, "because I was *stupid.*" Her eyes slitted dangerously. "You think every kobold *wants* to spy for the ice giants? It's just . . . a thing that has to be done along with every other chore, so we can keep our mines and our homes safe. There's no use *worrying* over it! If I'd been clever enough to listen to my family and realize I really might be caught, no matter *what* I did to protect myself—"

"Wait. Your whole family actually *threw you out*?" A growl battered behind Jasper's words as his neck curved so he could face her. "They didn't even try to protect their hatchling?" he demanded.

"What else could they do?" She flung out her arms, more agitated than I'd ever seen her. "They would have been frozen, otherwise—or stepped on! If anyone even *saw* any of them talking to me ever again—"

"But *you* weren't frozen," I said, "or stepped on. Wasn't

your crime even worse than theirs, according to the ice giants?"

"I don't want to talk about it," Fedolia snarled.

Smoke snorted out of Jasper's nostrils. "Family *doesn't abandon family*, no matter *what* stupid things they do."

*Ouch.* Those words made me shrink back in my seat, as I remembered my own sister's final words to me . . . and the way I'd run away from her afterward, without stopping to argue or apologize.

"Sometimes they do," I mumbled.

*But maybe they shouldn't.*

Jasper's family certainly never would. Jasper wouldn't even give up on *me*.

"You don't know anything about it," Fedolia repeated, more quietly this time. "But I'm taking care of my problems myself. So don't worry about it!"

She pointedly closed her eyes and pretended to fall asleep, her face tipped back to absorb the falling snow.

I could have forced her to admit she wasn't sleeping, but I was feeling raw, myself, as the hours passed and too many vulnerable memories swirled around me in the falling snow. I might have tried again later, but the moment that Jasper finally landed by a lake that evening, Fedolia blinked out of sight without a word.

I should have known that she still didn't trust me, even now.

"So much for getting any supper!" I sighed and slid off Jasper's back, landing on the snowy ground with a grunt of effort. "I suppose she couldn't have caught any fish tonight anyway." The lake that stretched in front of us under the star-lit sky, shadowed by massive, snow-covered mountains, was completely frozen over. It was an eerily beautiful sight, spar-kling in the stillness of the night, but a completely useless one for eating.

"I could melt through that." Jasper studied the thick sheet of ice with sleepily calculating golden eyes.

"But you can't catch fish. Remember?" Watching him try on our first morning had left all of us water-soaked, empty-handed, and laughing hysterically. "And if I try, I'll get frostbite. So ... we'll go hungry." *Again.* I sighed even harder and kicked melting snow away from his stomach to form a wet hollow that I could cover with my top two layers of clothes. At least I had practice at this, by now.

My teeth started chattering the moment I stripped off those outer layers. I almost purred with relief as I curled up tightly against Jasper's side a moment later. The heat from his scales steamed into my skin like the best, biggest hot brick in the world. *Bliss!* My stomach might be achingly empty, but at least I was warm.

I was beginning to hate the feeling of cold more than anything else in the entire world.

"It is *summer,*" I grumbled as I shifted to get comfort-able. "I don't care how far north we've come. Snow? Ice? This is ridiculous!"

Jasper let out a huff of smoke. "Can't you smell what's causing it?"

Frowning, I sniffed as hard as I could. All I smelled was *dragon*—comforting and familiar—and, much less comfortingly, my own sour reek, emanating through all my layers. The stench of sweat and grime had grown to an unbearable level after so many days of flying.

"It's not natural," Jasper said patiently. "It smells of magic."

"Oh." I huddled closer to his side. Suddenly, the big, frozen lake in front of us looked more ominous than beautiful. "Do you think it's the ice giants creating this weather?"

"It's been smelling more and more like them." A growl thickened Jasper's voice as he curled around me in a protective semicircle. "I'll never forget that scent."

We really were close now.

I wished Fedolia had stayed, whether or not she'd been able to catch us any dinner. Her air of careless superiority might burn, but I had to admit, I would feel better watching her treat this frighteningly magical landscape as a playground.

. . . Not that she'd done much of that since she'd spotted her family.

What memories were going through *her* head now, wherever she was hiding?

She might pretend not to need anyone's help, but Talvikki had been right. There was more emotion hiding behind Fedolia's glittering shield than I'd once thought. I *knew* I'd glimpsed real pain in her expression, even if she would never admit to it.

How difficult must it be for her to come back to her home after being expelled from it? To see her family and all she'd lost when they'd turned all their backs on her?

And why had she agreed to do it in the first place, when it caused her so much pain?

"A favor," I whispered to myself.

"I beg your pardon?" Jasper's purple-and-gold eyelids lifted, his voice sleepy and his big head propped on the snowy ground.

"Fedolia bargained to guide us," I said, "in exchange for me owing her a favor. Remember? I was just thinking . . ." Goose bumps prickled against my skin as Talvikki's remembered words echoed in my mind.

"*She's fond of tricks . . .*"

"I probably should have taken the time to ask her, first, what that favor would actually be."

Jasper's eyelids sagged closed as he visibly lost interest. "Does it really matter?"

I gazed out at the frozen lake and at the unnatural snow that fell steadily against it in the moonlight. Then I let out a sigh and let my worries fall out with it. "No," I admitted. "Probably not."

The truth was, there was *nothing* I wouldn't have agreed to for the chance to save my sister and finally—*finally*—get something right.

I would make the same bargain again in a heartbeat.

But as Jasper's snores grumbled through the long, dark night and Fedolia stayed worryingly invisible, my empty stomach twisted and knotted, and I wished—*how* I wished!— that my infuriating older sister were here to take control of me as usual.

I had a sinking feeling that I was about to muck up everything, again.

# CHAPTER 20

Fedolia flashed into view the next morning with a casual stretch and yawn just as I was staggering back from my makeshift chamber-pot trip. I was bleary-eyed with exhaustion and aching in every knotting muscle. She looked as fresh as if she'd slept peacefully all night long... which she probably had.

*Ugh.*

"Everything all right?" Jasper shifted to his feet, flexing his wings in anticipation. Smoke snorted in eager clouds from his nostrils, and his golden eyes gleamed as his front claws scraped impatiently against the ground.

Wait. Was he actually *hoping* for a fight?

He was! I could see it in his eyes. He *wanted* to prove himself as a fierce dragon, using teeth and claws instead of his brain. How could such a clever philosopher be so foolish?

"Of course." Fedolia's sharp teeth gleamed in her smile. She patted her hidden pendant with unmistakable satisfaction. "Everything's going perfectly."

"Ugh!" I finally let myself groan out loud. Was now *really* the time for her to gloat over her jewelry?

And could I *really* be the only one to realize we were heading to our deaths today—or at least to being frozen forever? I'd spent all night trying to think up a safe strategy, but there was no getting around the truth: there were only two ways we could possibly survive the day. Either we could melt and retrieve our families without a single ice giant noticing what we were doing, or I could magically transform myself into a perfect princess and negotiate their release with irresistible charm.

H*a!*

I'd always yearned to prove myself, too . . . but unlike Jasper, I could see exactly how any battle with ice giants would end.

So I was scowling as I stomped through the crackling white snow and hauled myself up onto my friend's back. "Well, then?" I growled, as snow-shards melted through my stockings. "Since there's no breakfast for us to eat before we leave . . ."

Humming cheerily, Fedolia hopped up in front of me. "I had breakfast," she informed us. "A snow hare! They're delicious. Nice and hoppy! You should try one sometime."

I couldn't even manage a groan at that. I just squeezed

my eyes shut and hung on with all my might as Jasper launched us into the air.

Fedolia was unbearably cheerful. As we soared over the vast white landscape, she kept up a running stream of commentary on every identical patch of snow below, sounding more excited than she'd ever been by any of the fabulous sights of Villenne.

". . . And that's where we used to go sledding when I was younger—oh, and *there's* where I always used to hide whenever I wanted to get out of work and my aunts were looking for me . . ."

*Wonderful.* Safely hidden behind her back, I rolled my eyes in disbelief. Did she really think this was a cheery little jaunt? She was showing off the barren world below as if she could convince Jasper and me to love it as much as she did.

We'd be fleeing it within just a few hours if we were lucky. If we weren't . . .

"Oof!" I let out an undignified grunt as Fedolia's elbow slammed into my shoulder. "What was that for?"

"You weren't looking, silly!" She pointed down with one long, blue-nailed finger. "You see? The ice giants' palace. We're almost there!"

"Where?" All I could see was a hint of blue shimmer on the horizon, like a long, low-hanging cloud, hazy and indefinable against the hulking, snow-covered hills and light gray sky.

"Just *look*," Fedolia told me firmly, and yanked my arms around her waist. Her invisibility spell snapped into place with a now-familiar *click*.

Jasper's wings swept us steadily through the air. A flash of pale light speared down through the heavy, snow-filled clouds ahead ...

And I sucked in a sudden, throat-scratching gasp as my vision adjusted, reframing every detail.

That blue shimmer was *ice*—not white and glacial and filled with rocks like the other big slabs we'd passed along the way, but tall and blue and impossibly translucent, stretching on and on before the low mountain range in perfect symmetry, like ...

*Walls*. Those were actual walls formed of magical ice! They marked out the borders of an astonishing structure. As we flew closer, I spotted massive rooms laid out within it, fitting closely around each of those snowy mountains. Only one thing was missing besides the giants themselves.

"Where's the roof?" I asked.

"Oh, Sofi." Fedolia shook her head. "Just look at those giants. Do they seem to mind the snow?"

"Where—*oh*." I gulped.

Those low, snow-blanketed mountains bordered by the walls of ice *weren't* mountains at all. They were the giants! They'd been covered with snow from head to foot as they knelt in perfectly eerie stillness within their translucent walls, as unmoving as any natural formations.

Human palaces were hives of activity and endless courtly schemes. None of these giants were scheming. They weren't even eating ... whatever ice giants ate.

They weren't talking or moving a single finger, either. They were just ... *there*.

"What are they doing?" I whispered.

Fedolia shrugged. "Waiting."

"For what?" Jasper growled softly.

Fedolia inspected one blue fingernail with deep concentration. "They aren't *terribly* fond of intruders," she told us. "So they sit there, and they listen, and they wait, and they watch . . . for as long as it takes. But they will never stop. Because they won't allow *anyone* to invade their territory."

"But they aren't doing anything with it!" I protested. "Look at them! They aren't even moving. Why should they care what other creatures want to do in other parts of it?"

"It's their *territory*," Jasper rumbled. "Of course they care."

"No, it's their *safety*," Fedolia snapped. "I thought you two actually knew something about ice giants by now!"

I would have torn out my hair with vexation if it hadn't been safely wrapped in four layers of warmth. "*You're* the expert, remember? We're trusting *you* to tell us about them and keep us safe!"

"Oh." Fedolia sounded uncharacteristically subdued. "Well . . . they . . ." Her right hand rose as if to touch the chain of her hidden necklace. Then she dropped her hand and gave her shoulders a quick shake. "*You're* the one who refuses to let anyone close," she told me. "You should understand them, if anyone does."

My whole body clenched with revulsion. "I do not!"

It wasn't *my* fault I didn't have any real friends except a dragon who lived beneath a mountain far away! It wasn't as if I didn't *want* to have friends.

For one brief, shining moment, I had even thought I'd

157

found some . . . before the ice giants came and ruined every-thing for me.

"Is this about their hearts?" Jasper sounded thoughtful. "I seem to remember—"

"I cannot believe we're worrying about their *hearts* when they're holding our families prisoner!" I shriek-whispered.

The safety of their hidden hearts might matter more to ice giants than anything else in the world, but that was *their* problem, not mine—and I had *nothing* in common with the monsters who had stolen Katrin.

"Who cares how they feel?" I demanded.

"Let's *not* worry about it," Fedolia muttered. "In fact, *please* don't talk at all, from now on!"

*Right.* I pressed my lips together, breathing shallowly through my nose.

Sitting utterly still, all day every day, these giants would hear a pin drop in their endless, wintry silence. But I couldn't spot my sister or any other captives amongst them . . . which meant their prisoners must be trapped on the other side of that unearthly palace.

To reach them, we would have to fly directly over the snow-covered figures as they sat, waiting and listening and watching for intruders.

"We are *definitely* invisible, aren't we?" I whispered.

"Of course we are!" Fedolia plucked irritably at the chain around her neck. "That was our bargain, remember? I keep you invisible all the way to the ice giants, and *you* owe me a favor. Simple!"

"Simple," I repeated numbly.

Thick, cold dread trickled through my bones as I stared at those looming, impossible shapes ahead. They seemed to grow more jaw-droppingly, mind-warpingly huge with every moment as we flew closer and closer.

I'd thought that the giants who'd stolen our families had been massive. But those must have been the young ones—the small ones, by comparison!

I could never charm these nightmarish creatures into anything. Who had I been trying to fool? I couldn't negotiate myself out of trouble with my own sister. I could barely keep the peace with my own best friend! I argued with *everybody.*

And that hopeful little plan of mine to rescue our families without any ice giants noticing?

*Hahaha!* Even locked inside my head, my laughter sounded hysterical. Out of control.

We were even closer now. They were *so* big. How could any living creature be so big?

The closest one had his eyes half-closed, but I didn't fool myself that he was sleeping. His massive blue-and-white face was set in rugged, watchful lines, as still and stern as if it had been carved from a stone cliff. Ice-tangled white hair hung from his head to his knees like a winter waterfall, mingling with the mountain-long beard . . . and he wasn't even standing up.

My breath stuttered desperately in my chest as Jasper's wings beat harder and harder in a final attempt to surmount that hulking shape. Higher, higher, *almost* high enough . . .

The ice giant's eyes flicked open, staring directly at us. Blue flames shone through falling snow.

*Aaahhhh—!*

My thoughts dissolved into a thousand whirling flakes of panic.

Jasper's wings started to beat hastily backward, but Fedolia poked his side to urge him on, her lips pressed tightly together.

My chest burned from lack of air. Jasper's big muscles quivered beneath us as he beat his purple-and-blue wings even harder than before. We flew steadily upward under that blue-flame gaze.

Thirty more feet . . . twenty . . . ten . . .

*There!*

My breath shot out in a ragged rush as he finally leveled out five feet above the giant's head.

In the distance, I glimpsed the far side of the giant's palace. There was something just beyond it, lower than the high, blue palace walls. Could it be our families' prison?

It was! It had to be.

*I'm coming, Katrin.* Relief gushed through my body as my gaze fixed on that distant point. Suddenly, I didn't care about danger or hunger or anything else.

*My sister* was waiting for me. I hadn't lost the last of my family after all!

Shifting my grip on Fedolia from her waist to her shoulders, I lifted myself into a crouch as we flew over the ice giant's broad head, squinting to make out more details. Was Katrin on the side of the slab closest to me? Or—

"Here we are!" Fedolia suddenly announced in a tight,

brittle voice. "We were invisible all the way to the ice giants, as promised!"

"Shh!" I hissed, still peering into the distance. "He'll hear y—!"

The invisibility spell vanished.

The giant just below us surged up with a terrifying, earth-shaking bellow. Jasper tucked his wings to his sides and shot forward, roaring furiously back at him. I tumbled back to my seat as an enormous hand launched toward us—and missed by only a foot.

Giants exploded from the ground around us like mountains launching into the sky. Carriage-sized blue-and-white hands grabbed for us. Ice shot through the snowy air.

Jasper dove between two jagged arrows of ice and lurched away from a third before it could slam into his side. Flame exploded in choppy bursts from his mouth as he scrabbled for balance in midair, flapping wildly.

"*Fedolia?*" Her name cracked in my throat as Jasper rolled and jerked beneath us. I clung to his scaly body with all my might. Bile rose up through my chest, but I forced it down, swallowing hard. "I don't understand—*why*—?"

"Sorry, Sofi." Her blue lips turned down in a grimace as she lifted her shoulders in a shrug. "I really am sorry, believe it or not. But I have a family of my own . . . and you should have made a better bargain."

# CHAPTER 21

Before I could even take in what she'd said, bluish-white skin filled my vision: a giant hand getting ready to close around us.

"Argh!" Screaming, I ducked.

Jasper dived downward, flipping to one side and taking us with him . . .

And I finally lost the battle with my stomach.

Fedolia shrieked as sick splattered across her blue robe and her long, beautiful, snow-white hair. Even that bluish-white hand retreated for a moment, jerking back in surprise at my unintentional sick-attack.

It was just enough to give Jasper a clear space to dive through.

*There!*

My stomach heaved all over again as he shot forward, but I hung on grimly, clenching my teeth together. Thank goodness I'd used myself up in my last round. Nothing came out of my mouth as I pressed my cheek against Jasper's hot scales—and Fedolia leaped to her feet in front of me, waving wildly.

"Stop!" Blue sparks shot from her fingers, and a cloud of blue mist puffed from her mouth as she balanced effortlessly on Jasper's moving back. "Don't hurt them!" she shouted. "They're valuable. I brought them here as hostages for you to freeze with the others!"

**"You!"** The closest ice giant's voice thundered through the air and shook my bones as he lumbered to a halt in front of us, forcing Jasper to stop just before we could slam into his granite-hard, blue-and-white stomach.

Flapping desperately, my one true friend fought his way backward while the giant leaned over us, bearded face scrunching up into a scowl. **"We know you. Traitor kobold!"**

"I'm *not* a traitor," Fedolia yelled back. "Not anymore! See?" She pointed at me as I clung to Jasper's back and he shot a stream of useless flame against the giant's impenetrable skin. "This is the other princess of Drachenheim. You missed her when you rounded up the royals! She wanted to set your prisoners free. She would have done it, too, if I hadn't come along. She's so stubborn, she never would have given up! But I made sure to bring her to you. I protected your territory! So . . ."

She put one hand to the silver chain of her necklace and clenched it between her fingers as she finished in a suddenly fragile, uncertain tone: "Can I *please* finally come home now?"

**"You?"**

I had thought there could be no sound in the world worse than an ice giant's bellow of rage.

I'd been wrong. His deep, echoing laughter felt like the end of the world breaking loose around me. The other giants joined in, and Jasper roared at all of them, but his roar was drowned out by that endless, wicked laughter.

All that kept my eyes open through it was the sight of Fedolia's small, white face above me.

I would never understand that kobold. She had betrayed me and Jasper after all our time together. I could never, *ever* forgive her for it.

And yet, somehow, I couldn't bring myself to look away from the unshielded agony in her face as she doubled over, wrapping her thin arms around her body and huddling into herself under the giants' waves of mocking laughter.

**"After what you did,"** our giant finally thundered, **"what home did you imagine you'd have left?"**

"*My family.*" Fedolia's words came out in a broken whisper.

But the ice giant still heard them. **"Your family?"** The force of his shaking head sent gusts of snow billowing around us. **"You have no family now, foolish girl. The ice of our land will not support you. Every kobold mine closed against you long ago. None of your people will look you in the eye again. No, little traitor."**

His last, terrible chuckle sent shivers rippling through my body. **"You may have saved your life with your final theft from us, but you lost everything you loved forever—and you will never be forgiven for it."**

Fedolia's mouth opened and closed wordlessly as she stared up at him. Her hand fell limply away from the chain around her neck . . .

And I finally put the pieces together.

How could I not have seen it before?

"Fedolia!" I pushed myself up until I was sitting on Jasper's back, under the weight of the ice giant's chilly gaze. It took all my willpower, but I kept my own gaze fixed on Fedolia's suddenly hollow-looking face, which looked devoid of all the false confidence she'd worn like a shield ever since I'd first met her. "Jasper can't hurt any of these creatures with his flame, can he? Because they don't keep their hearts behind their skin?"

Her eyes looked glassy with shock. She didn't speak.

"Fedolia!" This time I used the tone I'd heard from every Villennese lecturer who'd interrogated a student caught sleeping. "*What is your answer?*"

"No!" Her head jerked up. She blinked rapidly, touching her chest as if for reassurance. "He can't. Only their hearts are vulnerable."

"In that case . . ." Wobbling, I scooted forward. Jasper vibrated with rage beneath me. Smoke panted from his nostrils as he curved his long neck around and fixed his clever golden gaze on me.

"Fedolia," I said quietly, beckoning her to lean down and listen, "do you remember what Talvikki told me when we first met in that lecture hall on Scholars' Island?"

"What?" She blinked down at me. More and more ice giants were gathering around us now in a towering, tight circle, blocking out nearly all the pale sunlight from above. Fedolia gave them a dread-filled glance before she turned back to me. "Why—?"

"Talvikki was the one who warned me . . ." I lowered my voice to a whisper. She leaned even closer and I continued, "Students always sneak the most dangerous things beneath their robes. So I should have known"—I braced myself—"that you were doing it, too!"

I lunged forward and yanked the silver chain around her neck as hard as I could. It snapped, leaving the dangling pieces in my fingers. She gasped and jerked away, landing on Jasper's long neck. An ice giant in the distance let out a sudden, outraged bellow . . .

And I pulled those broken silver strands with me as I fell backward onto Jasper's scales with Fedolia's big blue pendant clutched safely to my chest. It was a massive, cold blue crystalline chunk that looked like priceless topaz but felt surprisingly soft and yielding as it beat a steady pulse against my fingers . . .

Because, of course, it was actually an ice giant's heart: the *only* thing Fedolia could ever have stolen that would ensure her own safety from them forever.

"Guess what?" I shouted to the ice giants as I scrambled back up on Jasper's back, clutching my stolen treasure to my chest. "I've been studying philosophy on Scholars' Island!"

Fedolia darted toward me, her blue eyes blazing, but for once, I felt no fear. Dragons *always* protected their territory . . . and I knew that was how they defined their friends. As I held the beating heart high for the giants' viewing, Jasper swung his long neck in a sudden, sharp jerk that sent the little kobold sailing off her feet, into the air.

She screamed—but he caught her as she fell. His teeth closed around her long white hair and held her safely in midair, bare white feet kicking uselessly.

"You idiots!" she shouted up at both of us. "If you had any idea what you were playing with—!"

"I know the definition of true power." I directed my words at the enraged giants above us, who were all roaring in a wordless jumble of fury. "And I'm holding it in my hand *right now!*"

I had never been any good at playing the part of a charming princess. I should have known better than to think I could do it today. But Fedolia had been right about one thing: I was stubborn. And I wasn't too afraid to fight after all.

# CHAPTER 22

"**Give that back!**" The order echoed from every ice giant at once with the force of a thousand avalanches. It was deafening. Overwhelming. More than anyone could possibly hope to bear.

But I'd been inside a dragon's mouth, committed a terrifying crime, and flown across the world without a chamber pot. I wasn't hiding from anything anymore. "Give my sister back!" I shouted back at them. "Let all your prisoners go!"

"**Never!**"

"It's useless," Fedolia called as she dangled by her hair from Jasper's teeth. "They'd sooner let one of their people die than risk losing an inch of territory."

*Argh.* So much for that idea. Still . . .

"Step back!" I yelled, holding up the beating heart.

"Or I'll get my friend to set fire to this heart right now. I mean it!"

Their roars were even louder this time than before . . . but the snow-covered earth shook beneath the ice giants as they each took a heavy, reluctant step backward.

*There.* There was just enough space for Jasper to fly through. But if they watched us fly away, they'd surely follow until we were off their territory—and that wouldn't work for me at all.

I only had one strategy left—and it relied on the one person I knew I couldn't trust. She'd played more than one trick on me already.

"Fedolia," I said, "unless you want Jasper to drop you to your death, you'll cast your invisibility spell over all of us. *Now.*"

She narrowed her eyes up at me. "You'll want to let me back up where you can touch me, then, won't you?"

"No!" I snapped. "You're not fooling me again." My tutors had taught me to memorize even the smallest details. I should have had more faith in my memory of this one. "Ever since we first took flight together, you've been pretending we need to touch for you to cast that spell, but I remember my first day in Villenne. As long as we all form a chain, you'll be fine.

"I think it's more work for you to do it that way—and apparently, you don't think we're worth the effort"—I bit out the words with an icy snap—"but I'm touching Jasper, and he's touching you. So we're ready, and I am *finished* with your games. I like you exactly where you are!"

"Stupid, sharp princess. I *told* Talvikki not to trust you."

Angry blue sparks puffed out from Fedolia's lips as she glared up at me . . . but the invisibility spell snapped into place a moment later.

I might be a useless princess, but I wasn't such a useless *person* as I had once thought, after all.

The ice giants started forward.

"Stop!" I yelled. "And *move away*, or you'll kill your friend by stomping on his heart with your big, clumsy feet!"

Grumbling with displeasure, they moved slowly backward, more space opening up between their looming bodies. Jasper shot through the closest crack with Fedolia swinging below his mouth.

*Phew!*

Fedolia crossed her arms as she sailed through the air and scowled up at me . . . but she didn't utter a single word. Whether we were friends or enemies, not one of our trio wanted the giants to see us now.

So Jasper curved his way above them with only the tiniest flicks of his scaled wings, and I kept my own mouth firmly closed as we glided across the vast blue palace. The slabs of ice beyond grew clearer and clearer with every moment.

There were so many small figures trapped within them, wearing gorgeous, rich colors that showed through their transparent prisons. There—I saw as Jasper curved around another lumbering ice giant who had blocked my view—was Jasper's own mother, terribly still, her blue-and-gold jaw outstretched in endless rage within her icy cage.

Jasper didn't roar when he saw her. His long jaw clamped

shut. But a trail of trembling white smoke escaped his nostrils, and his golden eyes looked wild.

In the slab just beyond . . . I sucked in a harsh breath, my pulse suddenly hammering against my wrists.

Katrin had never looked small to me before. Whenever she moved or spoke, my older sister took command of every space.

But she wasn't moving anymore. Dwarfed beyond Jasper's mother with one hand held out in endless, unmoving supplication . . .

She looked helpless. She looked *fragile*.

She looked agonizingly like our mother.

Jasper swung his head around to face me. He didn't need to speak for me to know exactly what he wanted. I remembered his words back in Villenne. *"What kind of dragon lets his mother be captured without a fight?"*

"No!" I hissed. My fists knotted so tightly that pain shot through my body. *"Keep on flying!"*

Dragons never left their families behind, and I truly loved their fiery loyalty. But I'd learned from my own, colder family that sometimes, hard decisions had to be made. Acting on impulse wouldn't help anyone right now, not with the ice giants on alert and awaiting our attack. First, we had to find a safe hiding place and gather information for a next attempt . . .

And I knew exactly who to ask.

Fedolia's gaze was deliberately averted from us both as she stared pointedly into the distance, her expression pinched. But I was aware of her silent presence at every moment as we flew past the ice that trapped our families and kept on flying, leaving them to fade, smaller and smaller, behind us.

It was unbearable. It was *wrong*.

By the time Jasper finally landed in a snow-covered valley within a tall mountain range twelve miles away, I was so far past my breaking point, I couldn't hold myself back any longer.

"Aaaaaarrrgh!" The desolate scream ripped from my mouth.

Dropping Fedolia to the snowy ground, Jasper tipped his neck back and roared out his own rage and fury. Hot orange flames shot high into the snowy air.

"Hmmph!" Dusting herself off, Fedolia picked herself up and shook her head up at both of us. "If you two *want* to let them know exactly where we are ..."

"We are *finished* with your directions!" I dropped off Jasper's back in one long jump, tossing him the ice giant's heart and landing hard on the thick snow. It crunched around my legs as I stomped forward, pointing at the kobold accusingly. "And you said *humans* were untrustworthy. Traitor!"

"I haven't betrayed anybody. Not this time!" She crossed her arms. "I fulfilled our bargain *exactly* as we agreed it. Is it my fault you didn't think it through?"

I clenched my jaw as Jasper's long tail lashed beside me, sending snow flying through the air. "I wasn't thinking clearly at the time," I snarled, "because my kingdom had just *lost its crown princess.*"

"And I lost my whole family! Wouldn't you do anything

to get *your* family back?" She pointed accusingly at me. "Isn't that what you're ready to do right now?"

"No!" I said tightly. "I'd do *almost* anything. But I wouldn't betray my own friends for it."

"Don't make me laugh! You were *never* my friend, and you know it, *Princess* Sofia of Drachenheim." Fedolia shook back her long, white hair and glared at me, balancing her light body on top of the packed snow with ease. "You didn't care about me or anyone else in Villenne. You didn't even tell us your real name!"

I winced as the blow struck home. "I didn't lie about it, though. My name *is* Sofia, just like I told you. I just . . . didn't mention all the other details."

"Hmm." A growl still rumbled deep in Jasper's throat, but as usual, philosophy functioned as a distraction. "Gert van Heidecker says that a lie of omission, intended to deceive, is as unethical as a statement of mistruth."

"Exactly!" Fedolia gave me a triumphant look. "And you knew *just* what you were doing when you introduced yourself to us the way you did, wearing clothes that couldn't have belonged to you."

"Yes, but I was only—"

"Putting your own needs first," Fedolia finished with satisfaction. "*Just* like me!"

"Argh!" I scooped up a cold ball of snow and threw it hard into the distance. "It is *not the same*. None of *my* secrets could hurt you!"

"You don't think you already hurt me?" She glared at

me. "What about the others? Talvikki always sang your praises. *She* said you showed that humans could be honest and trustworthy after all. You were *supposed* to be the final proof that we could make a real home for ourselves down south. But you were lying to us all along!"

"That is *not how it was*," I said through gritted teeth. "I wasn't trying to deceive you. It was just too dangerous to let anyone know—"

"It was only dangerous if you didn't trust us! We thought you *liked* us. The other girls all said you were our friend. I was even starting to believe it! But it was only a game to you all along—an adventure to entertain a bored princess on holiday. Our group never meant anything to you!"

"It meant *everything* to me." I was panting with the force of my frustration. "How can you not see it?"

"The moment you told us who you really were," she snapped, "I could see exactly how pointless it had *all* been— every lie I'd ever told myself from the moment I was thrown out of my home until the moment *you* made me realize no human would *ever* treat me with real respect.

"There is no use in trying to fit in anywhere except the place I was born, no matter how much I hate the ice giants' orders. So . . ." She jerked her pointed chin high in the air. "If you don't like the way I handled things, princess? You have *only* yourself to blame!"

I stared at her. She stared back.

Then Jasper gave a low, growling *hrrumph*, turning the ice giant's blue heart round and round in his claws.

"Actually," he said thoughtfully, "it's not *all* her fault, you know. It all comes down to the princess problem."

"Oh, for—!" I threw my arms up in despair. "We're back to this nonsense again? *Really?*"

Neither of them paid the slightest attention.

"She thinks she's responsible for her entire kingdom," Jasper told Fedolia.

"*Because I am!*" I bellowed. "How is that not obvious?"

"She thinks if she ever lets herself make a mistake or trust the wrong person, everyone else will suffer for it."

"*Because it's true.*" How could he not see it?

"And she thinks she's not allowed to truly care about anyone else because it might betray her kingdom."

"*Wrong!*" I said. "Ha! Princesses are *supposed* to care about their people."

"Oh, really?" He snorted out a cloud of smoke as he finally turned to me. "Then why won't you even admit that you love your own sister?"

My whole body flushed hot, then cold, at his question. Tremors swept through me.

Katrin's vulnerable, fragile figure, so like our mother's, trapped in the ice as we'd left her behind . . .

"We're not like other families," I bit out. "That's not how we think about things."

"No?" Jasper cocked his head like a professor encouraging a slow-thinking student. "So you never even loved your own parents? Really?"

It was too much.

"Of course I loved my parents!" I shouted. "But they *left* me! Mother died and Father stopped caring—and *that's* what happens whenever I let anyone close!"

Fedolia's mouth dropped open.

They both stared at me.

Suddenly, I felt overwhelmingly exposed, despite all my layers of stolen clothing.

Jasper's big head tilted to look down at Fedolia. Fedolia looked back up at him.

"Huh," she said. "You were right, dragon-boy. She may be a princess, but she definitely has problems."

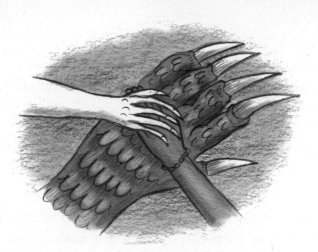

# CHAPTER 23

Unlike Fedolia, I couldn't turn myself invisible. I could only turn my back on the others and stomp ten pointed feet away to stand alone in the snow, my fists clenching and unclenching as waves of shame and fury rocked through me.

They murmured back and forth to each other behind me, voices pitched too low for me to make out their words. Maybe they were comparing notes on how quickly I'd lost my temper . . . again. Or maybe they were discussing what a failure I was at friendship . . . or bringing up other flaws that I hadn't even noticed.

How could Jasper join Fedolia against me when she'd *just* betrayed us both?

I *hadn't* betrayed her first.

Had I?

Talvikki had been so quick to forgive my deception that I'd let myself give up that unease straightaway. But now . . .

Oh, *argh!* It didn't matter how hard I tried. I always got *something* wrong.

But this time, I couldn't run away from the consequences, the way I had after my last soul-shattering fight.

So I drew long, cold breaths through my teeth and waited for the frantic chaos in my head and in my chest to subside as my skin grew colder and colder with every moment. I finally forced myself to turn around . . .

. . . And found Fedolia standing behind me, looking pensive.

"So," she began.

"Wait." I sighed. "I'm sorry," I told her. It was only the third time in my life I'd willingly uttered any apologies, but this one came out with barely a catch in my throat. "You were right," I admitted. "I should have told you and the others who I really was. I couldn't do it at first—it wouldn't have been safe or fair to my guards to put myself in any more danger. But once we became friends, it was wrong of me not to share the truth with all of you."

Fedolia's eyes widened. "Well," she said. "I wasn't expecting that."

"But that's not all." I swallowed over my parched throat, shivering hard. "Ever since I was born, people have only seen me as a princess, not as Sofia. They see the crown whenever they look at me—and honestly, they wouldn't like me at all if it weren't for everything I stand for, as a political symbol."

"That's—"

"That's why, when I was with you and Talvikki and the others, I was so desperate *not* to be a princess. I just . . ." Awkwardness nearly choked me, but I forced the words out anyway. "I just wanted you all to *like* me—for myself, not because of my family."

"We did." Fedolia frowned. "You *know* Talvikki and the others did—and I wanted to, by the end."

"But you were all thinking of me as a symbol, too." I looked her in the eyes, willing her to see it. "You just told me I was supposed to be proof that humans could be trustworthy."

"So?" Fedolia's frown deepened.

"You can't count on me for that. I get things wrong *all the time*! But that's because I'm a person, not a *thing*—and that's not something I can change to make anyone else happy. Believe me, I've spent my whole life trying!"

I glanced past her at Jasper, whose friendship I'd unfairly mistrusted for so long. I'd been so afraid he would see my flaws if we ever met in person—but instead, he'd seen right through them into my heart. "*That's* the real princess problem," I admitted. "It's everyone—including myself—thinking I can never make a single mistake, *ever*, or else I won't deserve anything at all . . . because only perfection is acceptable for a princess."

I looked back at Fedolia. "Jasper was right about you, too," I told her quietly. "Your family should *never* have given up on you just because you did one thing they didn't like.

That's not your mistake, that's theirs. *Dragons* wouldn't discard their hatchlings for being imperfect. None of the rest of us should, either. So . . ."

I drew a deep, snow-dusted breath, finally letting go of some of the fears that had clamped me tight for so long. "I can forgive you for betraying us," I said, "if you can forgive me for betraying you, too."

Fedolia didn't speak for a long time, as the cold wind blew between us. Then she jerked her chin in a brisk nod. "Fine," she snapped. "We can try to be real friends after all, I suppose . . . *if* you don't lie to me from now on. I won't hand you over to any more giants—and neither of us will give up on each other for any stupid mistakes we make along the way."

"It's a bargain." I couldn't hold back my smile.

The kobold in front of me was sharp-tongued and tricksy—*definitely* imperfect, just like me—yet, for once in my life, I felt absolutely no doubt about my own decisions as her lips quirked into a hesitant smile in return.

In different ways, Talvikki and Jasper had both pushed themselves past all my prickly, protective shields with their warmth and confidence to wrap themselves around my heart and turn me into their friend. Now, I could almost glimpse Fedolia's own hidden heart behind all her careful layers of glittering carelessness . . . and that glimpse was worth opening up my own shields at last.

Jasper said, "Well, I think we should all re-read Gert van Heidecker's lectures on the ethics of comradeship—with a bucket of hot chocolate—as soon as we get home."

Fedolia's smile vanished. "You two are going back to

Drachenburg? Well, of course you are. Obviously." She shook herself and took a quick step backward. "Anyway! I'll guide you as far back as Villenne, and then—"

"Oh no," I said. "We're not leaving yet."

"Not without our families!" Jasper growled.

Fedolia let out a startled laugh. "In case you didn't notice, you cannot rescue them. I thought that had to be obvious even to you two by now!"

Hot black smoke snorted through Jasper's nostrils, dispelling the last traces of philosophical distance from his ferocious face. "I'll melt the ice around my mother if it's the last thing I do!"

"Then they'll freeze you halfway through," she snapped. "You *cannot* steal from the ice giants without being found out. You can trust me on that one!"

"I *do* trust you," I said firmly. "And I think we should make another bargain now to replace our first one—an honest one on both sides, this time. You'll help us try to rescue our families, and in exchange—whether the rescue works or not—I'll make you a full citizen of Drachenheim."

"*What?*" Her eyes widened. "But—"

"I know you lost your first home when you worked against the ice giants last time. This time, though, you'll earn a home with me for as long as you want it. It could even be forever."

"Don't be ridiculous!" Fedolia's blue tongue flicked out to lick her lips in a quick, nervous swipe. "You know I'd never fit in at any royal human palace. I'd be the only kobold anyone's ever seen in all of Drachenheim!"

"So?" I shrugged. "I've never fit in there, either. I told you—no one there likes me much."

"But—"

"It won't be easy," I said, "but we can make it work if we're both stubborn enough. Any other kobold or goblin who wants to escape from the ice giants can find their own home in Drachenburg, too. We'll give them all the official freedom of the city."

There would certainly be ructions and outrage at that news. No one was used to seeing non-human creatures in the streets of Drachenburg . . . but so what? I hadn't been used to it until I'd arrived in Villenne. The people of Drachenburg hadn't been accustomed to the sight of dragons overhead, either, but they'd eventually gotten used to it. It was long past time for *all* of us to open our minds and hearts to the outside world—because there were some things you could never learn by staying locked in isolation.

And everyone—*everyone*—deserved a safe home.

Fedolia took a long, deep breath . . . and then another. Finally, a familiar, mischievous grin tugged her blue lips upward. "You know I do like trouble. What exactly are you planning?"

"We'll go in with fire and claws," Jasper snarled. "Obviously!"

"*No!*" I scowled at him in exasperation. "That's the *dragon* problem in a nutshell. Gert van Heidecker would be ashamed of you!"

"How can you say that?" I had never seen Jasper so offended. His neck reared above me, tight balls of smoke bursting from his snout. "I've been studying his books for years! Every other dragon sneers at your puny philosophers, but I could quote every single line—"

"But you stop *thinking* like them the moment danger comes," I snapped. "Your family defines power as *flame and claws*, so that's what you fall back on whenever you get scared."

"I am *never* scared!" Jasper thundered. "I am a *dragon*. Dragons do not feel fear!"

Fedolia rolled her eyes pointedly. I had to stifle a choke of laughter.

It felt surprisingly good to have two friends here, after all.

"Anyway!" I turned my laugh into a cough. "We certainly can't handle this like princesses, either." If *that* had been possible, Katrin's attempt to smooth things over in the first place would have worked. "And we can't handle it like dragons or like kobolds, since neither of those strategies have worked with ice giants before. So . . ."

I looked from one of them to the other—two true friends who looked like polar opposites. There was just one thing that bound all three of us together. "We're going to handle this rescue like *philosophers*."

It was time to find out how much I'd really learned on Scholars' Island, after all.

CHAPTER 24

The last time we'd flown toward the ice giants, fear had almost overwhelmed me. This time, I wrapped myself in the protective power of the emotion I'd struggled to resist all my life: un-pretty, un-princess-y *anger*.

These hulking creatures had stolen my sister. It was wrong, and I was *never* going to let it go!

"Hey! You lot!" I bellowed the insolent words as Fedolia dropped her spell of invisibility and Jasper landed us on top of the first icy prison-slab, where several of the ice giants had gathered in our absence.

"Ah-ah-*ahh*!" I waved the beating blue heart high in warning as giants roared to their feet all around us. "Careful! You don't want *this* to get hurt, do you?"

It seemed to take forever for the deafening roaring to

subside. But if they thought they could intimidate me now, they were wrong. I kept the same unimpressed sneer on my face until the noise finally died down.

"We are here," I shouted to the giants when they finally settled, "to discuss your plans for the future."

"**Stupid!**" An ice giant to our right shouldered past the others with a grinding noise, like mountains scraping against each other. His endless blue-and-white beard bristled to a halt six feet in front of me, jagged shards of ice sticking out like crystal spears of warning.

He'd already taken away my only family. He couldn't threaten me with any worse.

Fury gave me the strength to smile patronizingly up at him. "*You* know. Your plans to keep your precious little territory safe! That's all that matters to you, isn't it? We thought you might like the advice of trained philosophers while we're here."

He glowered down at me, raising one enormous fist in warning. "**No advice needed from tiny trespassers!**"

Jasper's big snout fell open in outrage. "What do you mean, *tiny*?!"

"Shh, dragon-boy," Fedolia muttered to him. "Brains not fire this time, remember?"

Ignoring them both, I crossed my arms. "No?" I asked the giant. "What *are* you planning to do, then, once all these rulers' armies start to arrive? Thousands and thousands of humans marching across your perfect, pristine landscape, messing up all that beautiful, flat snow . . ."

It took even longer for the irate roaring to subside this

time. Finally, the ice giant in charge—I thought of him as the Big One—cut off the others with a sweep of his arm that sent cold wind billowing through all my layers.

**"They send armies, we kill their kings!"**

"Mmm," I said doubtfully, turning to the others. "Do we really think that would work?"

Before I'd gone to Scholars' Island, I might actually have agreed.

Now, Fedolia shrugged. "There can always be new royals, can't there?"

"There can." I sighed. "Trust me, there are *always* more cousins lying in wait to take the throne the moment anything goes wrong." Personally, I couldn't stand any of my cousins—even Katrin could hardly bring herself to be polite to some of the really slimy ones—but still . . .

"As far as most people are concerned," I told the giants, "it doesn't actually matter who's the king. All they care about, deep down, is that there *is* one, just to serve as a symbol for the country. The crown is all that really matters, and there's always *someone* ready to wear that."

The Big One turned to the others. **"We'll send our scouts to take their crowns!"**

*Argh!* "That is not what I meant!" I shouted. "It's not about the *physical* crown, you idiots. It's just about someone *being in charge.*"

"Ice giants are very literal." Fedolia dusted off her sparkling blue nails. "You may be noticing that by now."

"*Dragons* don't wear crowns," Jasper growled. "And there

isn't a threat in the world that could stop my family from attacking if you keep my mother prisoner!"

The Big One glowered down at us, beard quivering. **"We're not afraid of puny dragons!"**

Dark smoke burst from Jasper's nostrils . . . but he kept his snout firmly shut, despite the look in his eyes.

I was *so* proud of my friend's true strength—but I had no time to stop and praise him for it.

"You might not be scared of dragons," I told the Big One sternly, "but do you really want them flying over your territory all the time to bother you? And as for the armies, they will *just keep coming.* There are so many humans in the world nowadays! They're all obsessed with looking powerful to each other . . . so they can't sit back and just give up when someone kidnaps their rulers and makes them all look stupid."

The Big One's beard moved up and down with the workings of his massive jaw, as if he were physically chewing over what I had said.

I decided to make it easier for him. "Let us take a moment," I said in my best lecturer's voice, "to consider the definition of *true power.*"

Fedolia chortled happily as she crossed her legs on Jasper's neck, settling in to get comfortable. "Let's hope this ends the same way the last lecture on power did!"

It was astonishing how easy it was to make someone listen to your philosophical opinions when you were holding their literal heart in your hands. Of course, it might have been considered cheating by a truly ethical philosopher, but I thought it was only fair: they were hold-ing my and Jasper's hearts, too, with our relatives trapped in their prisons of ice.

So I kept talking and talking . . . and talking even more, as my throat grew more and more parched with every minute, and Jasper and Fedolia took turns, too, to add their own thoughts on the matter.

The giants rumbled and bellowed, but they didn't walk away . . . and I took it as a good sign, two hours later, when the Big One's closest neighbor lifted up his great beard in response to my latest dry, hacking cough. A stream of cool, melted ice trickled down into my mouth a moment later.

I'd never in my life hoped to drink an ice giant's beard water. But my throat was in such dire straits by then that I swallowed down the cold, bitter stream with gratitude, tip-ping my head back to catch it all before I moved on to the next stage of my logical argument.

The Sofia I'd been a month earlier would have been hor-rified to find me here: dirty and rumpled, wearing multiple layers of stolen clothing and arguing with terrifying giants hundreds of miles away from the safety of my bedroom. I hadn't even tasted a sip of hot chocolate in weeks!

For the first time ever, though, I was filled with the glowing certainty that I was *exactly* where I belonged and doing what I had been born to do.

It felt utterly exhilarating.

Almost four hours after we'd begun, the Big One sighed heavily and shook his head, circling back once more to the main point that I'd driven all along. **"They will never stop coming? Even though they'd all die?"**

"Never," I said firmly.

"Trust her!" said Fedolia. "She's an *expert* on human stubbornness. Just look at her now!"

I was too tired to even frown at her by that point. I kept my weary gaze fixed on the blue-flame eyes of the Big One. "Whether you freeze thousands and thousands of soldiers or you kill them all . . . is that *really* what you want for your territory? A land littered with thousands of human bodies?"

The blue heart in my lap pulsed in time with my heartbeat as I waited for his answer.

**"Kobolds say,"** said the Big One at last, **"humans are coming anyway. New machines from their exhibition want to tear and change our land forever!"**

"I know what your spies in Villenne told you," I snapped, "but can't you see? Now's your chance to change that balance of power for good! The king of Valmarna only wanted to prove himself to the world by conquering the elements and creating new settlements here. But just think: what's even stronger than the elements? You are! You *control* the elements, for goodness' sake."

I waved at the magically icy landscape. "Valmarna and the other kingdoms will *never* stop attacking if you make them look weak to the world. But if you make them look strong instead—"

**"We're not giving up our land!"** Flames blazed in the Big One's eyes.

Jasper rumbled with reluctant sympathy.

"I *told* you they'd never go for it," chirped Fedolia.

"They don't have to." I smiled fiercely at the Big One. "I have a plan that will work for *all* of us," I told him, "but we'll have to melt my sister first."

# CHAPTER 25

It took *forever* to melt that ice giant's thick skull into thinking differently. Luckily, I had never been someone who gave up on an argument only because everyone else had already declared it useless.

A full hour after I'd first proposed my simple, sensible solution, the Big One turned back from his huddled comrades with a frosty sigh and a nod of resignation.

"**Fine,**" he boomed. "**But only if you stop talking. Which one is your sister?**"

Jasper jumped to his four feet and shook out his wings, nearly bouncing me off his back. "I'll melt her for you!"

"*No!*" I hadn't talked myself hoarse for the last five hours only to see Katrin's skin scorched by dragonfire now. "Our *hosts* are in charge," I said firmly. "This is their territory. Remember?"

Grumbling, Jasper lowered his wings, and I scooted myself back into place behind Fedolia. All together, we flew to the snowy ground just in front of my sister's prison.

Katrin reached toward us through the ice with her brown eyes widened in unending, desperate appeal, her slim figure looking tiny by comparison to the massive dragon whose jaw was open in a ferocious snarl just behind her.

A low, ominous growl rumbled through Jasper's long throat.

"Wait!" I whispered. "She'll come out next. I promise!"

My breath shortened into shallow, unsteady pants as I slid off Jasper's back and stood in front of the block of ice, gazing into my older sister's frozen eyes. Four feet of transparent ice separated us.

My heart thrummed against my chest.

Out loud, I said to the Big One, "This one. She's mine."

Fedolia let out a snort from her perch on Jasper's back, where she held the blue heart carefully cradled in her crossed legs. "Now you sound like a dragon!"

*Good.* I kept my eyes fixed on Katrin's face as the Big One held out one massive finger . . . and the ice *finally* began to melt between us.

Bitterly cold water eddied around my ankles. I didn't so much as budge to avoid it. I didn't dare look away for even a second.

*Hold on, Katrin!* I ordered silently.

She'd held on to our whole kingdom for years since Mother had died. She could hold on a minute or two longer.

Ice melted away from her figure, my breath caught . . . and Katrin let out an explosive cough and then spluttered, her eyes finally falling shut. Her body tipped forward helplessly.

I caught her before she could fall, grabbing her arms tightly. It was the first time I had actually touched her in years.

Her skin felt cold and wet and clammy—but I tightened my grip, and I didn't let go.

Slowly, her eyes reopened. "So . . . fia?" Her voice cracked, and she coughed again.

"I'm here," I said firmly, "and you're going to be all right."

For a moment, she just looked at me, wide-eyed. Shivers wracked her tall body. Her teeth chattered.

"Quick!" I said. "Jasper, warm her up."

He shuffled sideways obligingly, and she gave a violent start of surprise as his big, purple-and-blue body appeared before her.

"Come on," I said briskly. "Lean in! It helps."

"Sofia . . ." She clenched her teeth together, but she couldn't stop her shivers. It was the most out-of-control I had ever seen her—except, of course, when she'd lost her temper in Villenne.

"Oh, give in!" For the first time in our lives, I was stronger than my sister. I dragged her with me until we were both safely wrapped under Jasper's big wing, soaking in the glorious heat from his scales. *There!*

Her eyes fell shut. She took a long, slow breath, her jaw visibly relaxing. For one long moment, everything was silent, safe, and absolutely perfect.

Then she cleared her throat and pulled away from me with a yank as her eyes snapped open. Her gaze traced over my bizarre layers of clothing and the thick layers of grime on my skin with mounting horror. "Sofia, what in the *world* is going on here?"

*Now* we were getting back to normal.

"Um." Her accusing gaze dried up the words in my throat. "Well. Ah. The thing is . . ."

"Everything going all right in here?" Fedolia asked brightly. She peered under the curve of Jasper's wing and then sauntered casually in with us, carrying the heart in her arms. "Are we past all the boring kissing and hugging parts of the reunion now?"

Katrin's stunned gaze shifted from Fedolia's ghost-white face and long ears to the big, blue, pulsing ice giant heart.

"I told you," I muttered to the kobold, "we are not that kind of family!"

Katrin's eyebrows shot even higher at my words.

I couldn't bear to imagine what she was thinking. I ground my teeth. "I was just helping my sister warm up for a minute before she gets started with all the diplomatic bits!"

"I beg your pardon?" Katrin let out a choked laugh, turning back to me. "Perhaps, before I get started on anything, you could explain to me where we are and what's been happening?"

"Oh, *that*." Fedolia dropped to the ground and stretched her legs out comfortably before her, wriggling her bare white toes in the snow. "It's simple! The ice giants froze you and all the other royals and carried you off to their palace in the north. So Sofi dragged us all across the world to save you, and then she hammered them over their big heads until they agreed to let you go."

"*What?*" Katrin's jaw dropped open.

"That is not what happened!" Wincing, I edged away from both of them. "There wasn't any violence involved—not on our side, anyway. I just explained to them, in a perfectly reasonable way, that it would be much more sensible for them to let you go, and—"

"She lectured them," Fedolia said happily, "for hours. She wouldn't stop talking philosophy until they finally gave in. She is *so* stubborn!"

"She always has been." Katrin shook her head in what looked like wonder. "But Sofia ... how did you keep them from attacking you as well?"

"She blackmailed them with this after stealing it from me." Fedolia held up the ice giant's heart with unmistakable admiration. "She can be really ruthless, can't she? And she's getting much better at crime. Had you noticed that, too?"

"Not ... so much," said my sister faintly. "But I think I had better hear all about it."

Luckily, Katrin had always been a quick study. It only took her a few minutes to absorb the main details of what had happened and exactly what I had promised the ice giants so far.

"That's all perfectly acceptable," she said at last, "but I still don't understand one thing. Why did you need *me* to be melted first, for your plan to work?"

Wasn't it obvious? "Someone needs to talk all the rest of the royals into it."

"And you really think that 'someone' will be me?" She shook her head. "Sofia, have you even looked at me?" At some point during the recitation, she had sagged back against Jasper's side, and she was leaning all her weight against him now. "I have been frozen for nearly a week. I can barely even *think*, let alone stand upright long enough to persuade a dozen angry rulers into anything!"

"Don't be absurd." I scowled at her. "You can talk anyone around."

"So can you, apparently," she said dryly. "Otherwise, how would I be standing here right now?"

My jaw dropped. "You want *me* to talk to them? You *know* I don't have any diplomatic skills. They all despise me, anyway—and I already created one international incident!"

"But this time," murmured Katrin, "you'll be the strongest one in the conversation. And Sofia . . ." Her voice began to fade. "Power is *all* about perception. I learned that rule a long time ago. All you have to do now is make sure you use their perceptions to your own advantage."

"You mean—"

"You'll figure it out," she said quietly, her eyes falling closed as her head tipped wearily back against Jasper. "You're the one who studied at Scholars' Island."

There was something in her tone that I couldn't quite

pin down. Something that sounded almost like . . . *envy*? No. That couldn't be it, surely.

But as I watched her slide down Jasper's scales to the ground, her legs giving out beneath her, I had to accept the unpalatable truth.

My sister wasn't going to save us after all.

"Don't worry," Fedolia told me. "I'll look after her. You just deal with the other humans."

*Deal with the other humans?* I grimaced, remembering the last time I had *dealt* with them.

All the other humans in this group hated me! They thought I was positively feral—that I was the *wild* royal, which was a laughable proposition. They actually thought . . .

*Use their perceptions to your advantage.*

Katrin's words echoed in my ear, and I frowned.

The other royals thought I was the horrible, disobedient one, the one who might say or do *anything*.

So . . .

Oh. My eyes widened. Oh! I *could* use that.

Despite everything, a smile spread across my grime-caked face. I *loved* figuring out the answer to a really clever problem!

Jasper's mother was just as limp as Katrin had been when she first began to melt from her frozen state. But Jasper and I both shouted again and again in her ears, before she could even start to move, that the ice giants weren't our enemies anymore—that the people actually threatening her hatchling's safety now were the other human royals.

Protecting her hatchlings would always come first for

197

any dragon mother, no matter how much she might wish for fiery vengeance.

And it was amazing how much easier it felt to face the king of Valmarna ten minutes later, when I had two dragons looming directly behind me and the ice giants gathered all around us.

". . . So you see," I finished firmly as he finished coughing his way back into life, "this is a victory for *everyone*. The newspapers in Villenne will *all* claim you had a great success here, and everyone will be deeply grateful to you."

"They . . . will?" He blinked blearily at me, shaking his head . . . and then cringed, as Jasper's mother lowered her own head to give him a threatening golden glare. "But . . . look here, I told *everybody* we'd found new settlements, with farms and villages up north for them!"

"That was only a *threat*," I told him, "which you made in public to frighten the mighty ice giants into agreeing to a peace treaty with you. In exchange for staying out of their territory from now on, they will officially, *publicly* agree to never attack your kingdom again. Think of it! All the legends say no one could ever stop the ice giants—but *you* have, because of *your* Diamond Exhibition."

"I . . . have?" He blinked again.

"You have," I told him, "and the ice giants will say so, too, instead of stomping you right now . . . *if* you make the right decision. Your word is binding, my allies are your witnesses . . . and this is your only chance."

He looked up at the ice giants. He looked at the dragons.

Then he looked at me ... and apparently, what he saw on my grimy face didn't look like reassurance to him.

He really did think I'd stand by and watch him be stomped or burnt into ashes without a single word of protest.

I'd always thought it would be nice to be liked, the way my sister usually was—but I was finally starting to understand that being *un*likable held a power of its own.

"This is all most irregular, but I suppose..." He slid another uneasy glance at the giants, and his bushy gray mustache quivered. "If it really is for the good of my people, I mean..."

"You'll be known as the Peace Maker," Jasper offered helpfully.

"The Peace Maker?" His mustache twitched again, more cheerfully this time. "I do like the sound of that!"

The other royals all liked it, too.

They *especially* liked being released from their prisons while still being allowed to call themselves the winners ... and *not* being stomped or flamed in the process.

So it wasn't long before every kingdom on the continent had agreed to their first-ever peace treaties with the ice giants, which established the frozen north as a forever-untouchable territory ...

And that made the ice giants happy, too.

Most of the royals clambered onto Jasper's mother's giant back afterward, while she picked up four other royals with her claws. They would all speed together across the ice to return to Villenne as soon as possible—and to call a halt to any advancing armies they spotted along the way.

Katrin, though, stayed with me, Fedolia, and Jasper. Once her legs had finally regained their strength, she had emerged from the protection of Jasper's wings to stand and watch the whole proceeding with an unreadable expression. Now, as we waved away the others—after many stern instructions had been growled at Jasper by his mother, and many earnest promises had been made by him for good behavior on his way back—my sister turned to me with a look that said we weren't nearly done yet.

"Sofia," she said, "I think it's time that you and I have a talk of our own . . . in private, if you please."

Over her shoulder, Jasper gave me a sympathetic grimace.

Fedolia didn't even try to hide the warning "Ooh!" shape that she made with her mouth.

"Fine," I mumbled.

There really wasn't any excuse to put the moment off any longer.

Slowly and reluctantly, scuffing my feet in the snow, I followed my sister away from my friends to my certain doom.

# CHAPTER 26

All too soon, Katrin came to a halt. We were only fifteen feet away from Jasper and Fedolia when she turned to face me— and I knew for a fact that they were both watching us. I hated being told off in front of an audience! My back stiffened and my skin prickled with misery as I braced myself to endure it once again, *just* like I had back in Villenne.

Jasper and Fedolia already knew all my worst secrets, though. That was something that had never been true for me before. After all those years of scrambling to hide my imper- fections from everyone, it felt nigh on miraculous to have two friends who knew every one of my flaws—and liked me anyway.

Still, the pressure built up in my chest as I waited . . . and waited . . . and waited for my sister to pronounce judgment.

"So," Katrin finally began.

"I *know!*" The words burst from my mouth like an explosion. I flung my arms high in the air. "I know everything you want to say to me, all right? You don't have to go over all of it. I did *everything* wrong from the time I landed in Villenne. I was rude to their king, I ran away to Scholars' Island, I made the wrong kind of friendships—"

"And you just saved all our lives, including that pompous king's—with the help of the friends that you found on Scholars' Island." Katrin's head tilted to one side as she studied me. "Had you really not noticed that part? I did."

I glowered furiously up at her. I would *not* be fooled again. She was only trying to soften me up! She wanted me to *think* I was safe so that I'd relax my guard, and then she would immediately announce some horrible new mission or a terrible decision about my future marriage.

If she tried to betroth me to an ice giant, I would *not* agree to it!

"I know you'll never forgive me," I said bitterly. "I heard you back in Villenne, remember?"

"I beg your pardon?" Katrin gave a startled laugh. "Sofia, in case you didn't notice, I was a wreck when I arrived in Villenne!" She plucked at her crumpled gown and grimaced. "I had just spent *three days straight* being sick from morning until night, and I'd barely slept for worrying about you and our kingdom. How could I have ever made a sensible decision about anything under those circumstances?"

I wrapped my arms around my chest like a shield. "Your decisions are always sensible. Everyone knows that."

Her lips twisted. "So you think you're the only one who's ever allowed to make a mistake or behave irrationally?"

*Unbelievable!* "How can you say that?" I demanded, my arms falling to my sides. "You *never* let go of anything I do wrong! I am *never* allowed to be anything but perfect!"

"Oh no?" Katrin's voice took on an edge. "And how do you think I should train you instead? By telling you it's fine to be rude to powerful people? By *encouraging* you to make enemies and lose important connections?"

She shook her head impatiently. "You're a *princess*, Sofia. That means you'll be on display for the rest of your life, whether you care for it or not. I have to help you learn to hide your feelings and do whatever's necessary to survive court life."

"What do you care about my feelings?" Tears thickened my throat as I glared up at her, years' worth of pain boiling up at last. "When you lost your temper in Villenne, it was the first time you'd let me see any of *your* feelings in years. And your true feeling, when you weren't well enough to hide it, was that you don't want to be my sister! You've only ever looked after me because you have to, and I know it!"

Katrin lurched back as if she'd been slapped. "You have no idea what you're talking about!"

But I wasn't holding myself back anymore. "Oh yes, I do. Your promise to Mother." Salty tears burned my eyes. I wiped them away impatiently with my stolen shawl. "I heard her make you promise, at the end, to look after me." I shrugged bitterly. "Everyone knows you always keep your promises. But you have *always* made it clear that you didn't want to do it. I know I'm a horrible disappointment to you."

"Sofia . . ." Katrin sighed and closed her eyes for a moment. "If you'd only stop for a moment and calm yourself—"

"I can't!" I said impatiently. "I'm not a natural princess, the way you are, and you know it. Why did you even send me to Villenne in the first place? Were you really that desperate to be rid of me? You must have known I wasn't ready for that mission!"

Katrin's laugh sounded shockingly raw. "How do you think I learned to rule a kingdom at sixteen?" she asked. "Do you think I felt ready for *that*?"

She shook her head. "Sofia, I'm not a 'natural' princess, either. Mother trained me all her life until she died! But I was supposed to have years left to learn afterward. I was even trying to think up ways to attend university in Villenne myself!"

"*You* were?" I couldn't even imagine it.

She cut a dismissive line through the air with one hand, moving on. "*Of course* I didn't feel ready to take over at sixteen—not with the kingdom, and certainly not with you. That was never supposed to be my responsibility! Not until I was old enough to have children of my own."

My shoulders hunched.

"But who else was going to do it?" she asked. "*Father?*"

Our eyes met.

We both knew the answer to that question. Mother might have been the one who'd died, but our father—the one we'd known, the one who'd loved and looked after us—had left both of us just as permanently.

"I'm sorry," I mumbled. Shame gushed sickeningly through my skin, flushing me hot and cold in turn. I took a step backward. "I shouldn't have complained. I just—"

"No," she said, "that is *not* what I'm saying. My point is, I didn't know how to do that either! I'm trying my best, Sofia. But when it comes to raising you . . ." Her lovely face sagged. "Apparently, I always get it wrong. It seems to be inevitable."

She gave a bitter shrug as I stared at her, stunned speechless.

"I tried to teach you to shield yourself, to make you strong," she said, "and it made you think I didn't care about you. I pushed you to escape the walls of our palace, and you thought I was throwing you away!" Her laugh sounded unbearably sad. "I think we can both agree I'm hardly doing a perfect job at raising you."

"You were right, though," I said. "You shouldn't have to be doing it."

"But I want to," she said. "Can't you see?" Slowly, she took a single step toward me. Tentatively, she lifted one hand. "You're my sister, Sofia. Doesn't that mean anything to you anymore?"

I let out a choked laugh. "Why do you think I just flew across the world on dragonback?"

I didn't realize I had lifted my own hand. But suddenly, our fingers were touching in a butterfly-light connection. The slightest movement would have been enough for either of us to break the hold.

I kept my hand exactly where it was. Her fingers were longer and slimmer than mine, and they felt icy cold.

Jasper would never give up on his family. And I remembered the agony on Fedolia's face. "*Wouldn't you do anything to get your family back?*"

Her family had broken because they'd refused to forgive her.

I couldn't bear for us to do the same.

Slowly, I closed my hand around hers. Then I took a deep breath.

"I can't stand being manipulated anymore," I told her. "I *hate* it when you trick me into doing things. I don't care if you're doing it for my own good! It makes me feel small and stupid and useless, and you have to stop."

Her face tightened. She breathed in and then out through her nose without speaking. Finally, she opened her mouth and said, "I understand. But if you don't want me to trick you, Sofia, you have to actually *do* the work I ask. Help me run our kingdom. Don't make it even harder."

I wanted to snarl in self-defense. But I held my breath, counted through my first, instinctive pulse of anger . . . and let it go. "I'll try."

"Then so will I." She turned her hand in mine to squeeze my fingers.

We weren't the kind of family that did hugging or kissing. But a warm glow emanated down my arm from the point where our hands held each other.

Then realization hit. "*Wait.*" I gasped, dropping her hand. "Wait a minute!" All that talking about how she'd manipulated me for my own good . . .

"Those houses I'm building on the riverbank," I breathed. "They were *never* in any danger, were they? That was just your way of tricking me into flying to Villenne!"

"We-e-ell . . ." Katrin winced. "I wasn't being *untruthful,* exactly. The merchants weren't pleased about those new constructions . . ."

"But you'd never let them tell us what to do," I said, "so you talked them around, the way you always do . . . and then tricked *me* into thinking I had no choice but to fly with a dragon!"

"I had no choice!" Katrin said passionately. "You were hiding in your room! You'd barely left it for months! How else was I supposed to pry you out of your tortoise-shell?"

My lips opened to shoot back a furious retort . . . and a sudden flurry of snowflakes gusted into my mouth. I gagged, coughed, spat them out . . .

And let out a spurt of laughter as I looked at the snowy landscape around us and the massive, hulking giants I had actually forgotten in the heat of our argument.

"Does this really *look* like I'm hiding in a shell?" I asked my sister.

"Not anymore." She gave me a catlike smile of satisfaction. "I really do know what's best for you, don't I?"

"Ha." I narrowed my eyes at her. "Well, I know that a lie of omission, intended to deceive, is just as unethical as a statement of mistruth."

Katrin sighed. "I should never have let you buy all those philosophy books, should I?"

"Too late now," I told her happily, as we started back toward my friends. "And you'll have plenty of time to listen to all of us explain every one of those books to you on our way back to Drachenburg. It'll be the perfect punishment!"

# CHAPTER 27

I couldn't believe Katrin made us stop to visit the Diamond Exhibition on our way back home. But it wasn't only the exhibition that we visited. We swanned through every glittering soiree at the white palace in Villenne, dressed in the finest gowns our ladies-in-waiting had packed for us.

Katrin charmed everyone we met, as usual; I smiled fiercely at her side; and every time another royal made passing conversation with either of us, they were reminded of exactly which kingdom had saved them all from the ice giants' prison.

It was remarkable just how many new alliances we would take with us back to Drachenburg after all . . . and because I was trying to help my sister, I kept my mouth clamped shut through every tedious courtly evening, resigning myself to my royal duty.

On the fifth morning of our stay in Villenne, though, I woke to find my sister nudging my shoulder, with Fedolia smirking mischievously by her side. It was barely light outside the windows of my luxuriant palace bedroom, but Katrin was already fully dressed in a plain dark cotton gown that I'd never seen on her before.

"Hurry!" she whispered. "We have to leave early to avoid being seen."

"What do you mean?" I peered groggily up at her, blinking sleep crust from my eyes. "We're always seen. That's the whole point of this visit, isn't it?"

"Not today." Katrin looked suddenly years younger as she gave me a mischievous grin. "This morning, the princesses are both sadly indisposed . . . because I want you two to show me the university district."

My eyes shot wide open. "You do?"

Fedolia nodded confidently. "Don't worry," she told my sister. "Sofi and I can show you *all* the best places to go!"

And we did.

That was how I ended up in the underground coffeehouse four hours later with my elegant, perfect older sister sitting across from me. Her legs were tucked beneath her on a lumpy cushion, her fingers were wrapped around a bowl of hot coffee, and her expression was rapt as she listened to old Abjörn the troll—no longer sleeping—tell the whole coffeehouse how he'd turned vegetarian during his epic, thirty-year dream.

Sitting there with my two worlds blended together felt like a wild and unlikely dream itself. I kept waiting to wake up—or for Katrin to surge to her feet and demand that we leave before her dignity could be compromised.

But Katrin wasn't wearing her royal clothes today. She had wandered around Scholars' Island in a student robe with a distant, thoughtful look on her face. She had watched students her own age sprawl across the grass, and she had glanced into crowded lecture halls with what looked like wistfulness in her eyes. She didn't look in any hurry to emerge from our shared escape . . .

And shrieks of raucous delight sounded behind us as Talvikki, Hannalena and Berrit tumbled down the stairs into the room.

"Sofi!" Talvikki reached me first and flung her strong green arms around me while the other two flocked around Fedolia. "You survived—and you came back! Are you here to stay?"

Katrin turned to listen to my answer. But I didn't glimpse any hint of rebuke in her expression, only rueful sympathy. We both knew what I had to say. It had made every moment of today bittersweet and almost unbearably special.

Throughout every minute I'd spent walking around the big, ivy-covered brick buildings of Scholars' Island that morning, and then sitting in this dimly lit underground haven, soaking in all the extraordinary sights and sounds, I had known this would have to be my final visit. I had responsibilities waiting for me back home. I wasn't going to hide from them anymore—not in my own bedroom and not in a lecture hall in Villenne, either.

I'd always known that Scholars' Island was an impossible dream for me. But it felt startlingly right to share this final visit with my sister, who understood that dream better than I ever could have imagined.

"No," I said to Talvikki as I hugged her back with all my might. "We're only free from the palace for one day. But you can all come to Drachenburg any time to visit, *or* to stay for good—can't they, Katrin?"

My sister nodded, her gaze clear. "Of course," she said. "My sister's friends will always be welcome in our home—and you might let others know as well: Drachenheim is always looking for clever, hard-working immigrants to add their own unique strengths to our kingdom."

"We-e-ell..." Talvikki grimaced apologetically as she traded a skeptical glance with the other goblin girls. "We do appreciate the offer—but a city without a university of its own? And isn't Drachenburg only half the size of Villenne—or even less?"

Katrin's eyes narrowed dangerously. "You might be surprised by some of the changes coming to Drachenburg."

H*mm*. I suspected that the nobles and merchants who ran our city would be even more surprised—because I knew that look on my sister's face. I wasn't the only one who'd soaked in new information and ideas from the outside world.

Drachenburg had no idea what was about to hit it.

If she was thinking of founding a new university, I would make certain that dragons and goblins and kobolds were allowed as students . . . oh, and princesses, too, if their kobold friends kept them safely invisible whenever they sat in on philosophy lectures. We might even be able to persuade Gert van Heidecker to come and work there, too, once the stuffy king of Valmarna finally let him out of prison.

It was good to start coming up with possible dreams for the future, to begin to replace the old, impossible ones.

But it hurt horribly to wave good-bye to Talvikki, Hannalena, and Berrit an hour later. They were heading off on another wild adventure, planning to explore a newly discovered cave system under one of Villenne's farthest islands, and they planned to camp there overnight. I could already imagine just how much fun they would all have.

Fedolia was going with them, too, for one last expedition with her own first friends, although she would rejoin me and Katrin the next day . . . or the day after, if they all chose to stay a second night.

As the whole group disappeared up the staircase, their shriek-laughing energy vanished with them, leaving the coffeehouse feeling strangely quiet by comparison . . . and horribly flat.

Katrin looked at me across the makeshift table. Only a candle stub guttered now between us in its tarnished brass candleholder. "Is there anything else you'd like to show me?" she asked gently.

I took one last look around the long, dark room that had been my sanctuary—from the glowing blue-and-green moss on the walls to the goblin owners leaping fluidly up and down the shelves—and sighed.

"No," I said. "I think it's time to go back."

We didn't have Fedolia to make us invisible on the long walk back. Jasper couldn't be with us, either. He and his mother had already flown south to reassure their dangerous family that they didn't need rescuing after all. We'd barely even had a chance to say good-bye once we'd reached Villenne and he'd dropped us off at the palace.

"Don't worry," he'd whispered as I'd slid off his back. "I'm not letting myself be cooped up in the family cave again. We'll see each other very soon."

From the glint of determination in his eyes, I knew he meant it—and I knew he'd do it, too. Jasper had more strength than any of his family realized.

From the fierce look on his mother's face, though, it might be months before he won that particular battle. Even when he did come, it wouldn't be the same.

Everything about my holiday was coming to an end.

My feet dragged as Katrin and I walked side by side down the crowded streets, shielded from notice by our plain student robes. The people around us turned into a humming blur of background, color and noise washing over me as I trudged back toward reality.

Back home, I would never again be allowed so close to outsiders. I would ride through the city in our gilded, protected carriage, with glass windows and armed outriders keeping a constant wall between me and everyone else on the streets.

But I wouldn't forget what it felt like to share those streets. Not ever.

The guards at the doors of the white palace stared when they saw us walking toward them, but I didn't have the energy to think up any excuse for our outlandish outfits. My sister didn't bother to offer any. She only nodded graciously and waited for them to hold the doors open . . . which, after a flabbergasted moment, they did.

*Almost there.* Ten minutes later, we were stepping through the front door of our luxuriant guest suite, and I was counting down the steps until I could *finally* reach my bed and a comforting cup of hot chocolate, to escape from everything . . .

When an unexpected sound suddenly broke through the air.

"*Mrrrrow!*"

I spun around.

The door to my bedroom was closed, but something—someone!—was scratching at it madly from the other side.

"*Mrrow!*"

Lena and Anja came running from their room, their faces pink and suffused with excitement. "Aren't you going to open your door?" Anja demanded. "We've spent *days* searching for him! He's been waiting for you for hours!"

"*He?*" My lips formed the word, but I couldn't speak it out loud. I didn't dare.

"Oh, for goodness' sake." Ulrike heaved a put-upon sigh and rose from the couch where she'd been embroidering. A covert smile tugged at her lips as she stalked to the door. She turned the handle herself, giving me a sidelong glance.

The door swung open . . .

And a brown-and-gold blur shot out of it, leaping straight toward me.

"Ahh!" Katrin let out an unladylike yelp of surprise. "Sofia, *what*—?"

But I couldn't answer.

My cat had landed in my arms, and he was purring and purring, rubbing his big, soft head against the underside of my chin and scrambling up my chest uncontrollably. He draped himself around my neck like a velvety wrap of warmth and love, nuzzling my face again and again as I whispered, "*It's you, it's you. It's really you!*"

I didn't even realize I was crying until Ulrike, *tsking*, passed me a silk handkerchief. It was perfectly pleated, of course.

When I finally looked up after blowing my nose, I found *everyone* gathered around me: Lena and Anja, Ulrike and Katrin, and Jurgen and Konrad, too, beaming with pride.

"We've *all* been hunting," Anja explained to my sister. "He never had a real home of his own, you see, so—"

"He does now," I said thickly. Tears clogged my throat and nose, but my cat's steady purr resonated through me, and I kept one hand buried in his thick fur as I looked to my sister. "You said all my friends were welcome in our home. Remember, Katrin?"

My sister looked at me for a long moment, as my cat rubbed his soft face against mine again and again. Then she sighed and shook her head in resignation. "What do you call him? I ought to know how to address him if you're really planning to add *him* to your household as well."

"He doesn't have a name yet," I told her, "but . . ."

I looked at everyone around me. All of them were watching me and my purring, nuzzling cat with open pride shining on their faces.

I hadn't chosen any of my attendants for myself. I'd spent years feeling bitter about that—and punishing them for it, too, by shutting all of them out from my heart and my mind. But they'd been there for me anyway, through thick and thin, through cannonballs and dragon flights.

Some good things really did have to come to an end. But others—if I worked hard for them—might be just beginning. I looked, one by one, at each of my attendants and guards, who might all one day—if I was truly lucky—become friends.

"Thank you," I said softly. "Thank you. *Thank you.*"

Finally, I turned back to my sister as my cat nestled his head against my hair and purred deafeningly into my ears, wrapping his fluffy tail around me. "I think we should *all* choose a name for him together," I said, "on our way back home."

# ACKNOWLEDGMENTS

Thank you so much to my intrepid beta-readers, Patrick Samphire, Rene Sears, Aliette de Bodard, Tiffany Trent, and Jenn Reese.

Thank you to Tricia Sullivan for organizing the perfectly timed retreat that helped me figure out the right way to write this book, and thank you to Trish, Justina Robson, and Freda Warrington for an amazing experience full of support, encouragement, and really fabulous chocolate tarts.

Thank you to Jamie Samphire for asking me to read this book as his bedtime story as I wrote it and for always asking for more. Your encouragement made such a difference to me!

Thank you to Molly Ker Hawn for being the best negotiating partner any writer could ever have (and a rock of emotional support and good advice, too).

Thank you to Patrick Samphire for patiently reading every single draft of this book's opening and giving excellent feedback every time.

Thank you to Ellen Holgate and Sarah Shumway for caring about my characters and wanting more stories in this world. Thank you to Ellen and to Lucy Mackay-Sim for the thoughtful structural edits that helped me strengthen this book. Thank you to Sarah and to Claire Stetzer for shepherding it so beautifully into publication in North America, to Amanda Bartlett for careful and thorough copyediting, and to Susan Hom for fantastic proofreading. Thank you to Petur Antonsson for another beautiful cover, and to Jeanette Levy and Donna Mark for the fabulous cover design. And thank you to Erica Barmash, Anna Bernard, Phoebe Dyer, Beth Eller, Alona Fryman, Courtney Griffin, Erica Loberg, Brittany Mitchell, and Lily Yengle for marketing and publicity!

Thank you to all the philosophers who responded to my cry for help on Facebook with such thoughtful, fascinating responses: Ian Balzer, Dr. Ben Burgis, Dr. Bree Morton, Dr. Jennifer Burgis, Steven Barker, Annalise Harrison, Kaleb Earl, and Alexandra Roumbas Goldstein. (And thanks to Jasmine Stairs for helping me gather many of those responses!) I really appreciated all of them.

And thank you to every reader who has followed this series and helped my dragons fly. I wish I could make hot chocolates for every one of you!